FEB 27 2008

THE TURQUOISE DRAGON

The Turquoise Dragon

A MYSTERY

David Rains Wallace

A YOLLA BOLLY PRESS BOOK PUBLISHED BY

Sierra Club Books
SAN FRANCISCO

The Sierra Club, founded in 1892 by John Muir, has devoted itself
to the study and protection of the earth's scenic and ecological
resources—mountains, wetlands, woodlands, wild shores and rivers,
deserts and plains. The publishing program of the Sierra Club offers
books to the public as a nonprofit educational service in the hope
that they may enlarge the public's understanding of the Club's
basic concerns. The point of view expressed in each book, however,
does not necessarily represent that of the Club. The Sierra Club has
some fifty chapters coast to coast, in Canada, Hawaii, and Alaska.
For information about how you may participate in its programs
to preserve wilderness and the quality of life, please address inquiries
to Sierra Club, 530 Bush Street, San Francisco, CA 94108.

A YOLLA BOLLY PRESS BOOK

The Turquoise Dragon was prepared for publication
at The Yolla Bolly Press, Covelo, California,
under the supervision of James and Carolyn Robertson

LIBRARY OF CONGRESS CATALOGING IN PUBLICATION DATA
Wallace, David Rains, 1945–
The turquoise dragon.
"A Yolla Bolly Press book."
I. Title.
PS3573.A42564T8   1984   813'.54   84-5471
ISBN 0-87156-819-5

Cover illustration by Sandra Dean

PRINTED IN THE UNITED STATES OF AMERICA

10 9 8 7 6 5 4 3 2

To Robert Gerstenlauer

Acknowledgments

I'm grateful to Jon Beckmann for providing a little early sup-port to get this first fictional exercise off the ground; to Jon, Jim Cohee, Danny Moses, Diana Landau, and Carolyn Robertson for useful criticisms, suggestions, and encouragement; and to James Robertson for productive but relaxing story conferences in the Middle Eel.

D.R.W.

You live in a place full of light bulbs
and chrome and rare fillets and box top contests.
But when you die, you die in a place
of mountains and sky, earth and fire,
stars and the sea.

John D. MacDonald
All These Condemned

Chapter One

I HADN'T EXPECTED Tom Blackwell to be home. We are such busy people, busier all the time. I was in the city for just a day, doing a few errands. It was rush hour on one of those hot spring days when the smog spreads an orange pall across the bay. As I inched along the freeway, I saw the exit that led to Blackwell's apartment in north Oakland and turned onto it suddenly, the thought of a cold beer almost palpable in my mind. I had no reason to anticipate any such thing. I hadn't seen Blackwell in a while, didn't even know if he was in town. You have to follow an impulse occasionally. I drove around his block three times looking for a parking place and finally left my pickup by a hydrant.

Nobody answered the doorbell. Somehow it wasn't good enough. There'd been too much standing outside empty rooms in my life just then. I tried the door. It was one of those ground-floor, back-door apartments, at the end of a passageway over-shadowed with acacia, toyon, and deodar. A private place. I tried the door, feeling a bit slimy, and it opened.

I thought he was asleep, on a Mexican wool rug, with watery traces of afternoon sunlight on his legs. Even when I saw the black stain on the white wool, my mind refused to produce the appropriate concept. I must have looked the way a dog does when it's sniffing another that has just been run over.

13

How many pictures of corpses does the average civilized person see in a lifetime? I know I've seen thousands since those first grainy photographs of decapitated Chinese bandits I found in an ancient *National Geographic* on my second grade bookshelf. I'd seen one just the night before on my local TV station. The corpse had been in an orchard (I live in the country). It hadn't seemed particularly unpleasant, but then I don't think they'd have shown it on television otherwise. There hadn't been much left but the clothes, a pair of chinos and a varsity jacket. The rest had gone the way of the bluebottle fly. I'd felt a certain sneaky satisfaction. One less contender for breathing space.

It hadn't prepared me for the real thing. Pictures don't smell. It wasn't the smell of dead animals: I know that well enough. It was the smell of blood, and shit. Blackwell had been alive very recently. I'd have preferred a skeleton, or maybe even something swollen and maggoty. He looked too much like *me*.

I stepped back through the door and closed it. I wondered if I should wipe my fingerprints off the doorknob. I'd entered illegally. I thought it might be best just to go away. He could have been run over by a bus or gotten cancer or disappeared into the Amazon.

But was he really dead? For sure, with all that blood on the rug, he was dead. But had I left prints on the *inside* doorknob? I opened the door and crept back in. I made myself squat and look at his head. A familiar face, but bruised, puffy, pale. No blinking, no twitching of nostrils, no rise and fall of the shoulders. Stillness, except for a couple of complacent flies.

The hole in the back of his head wasn't very big, was barely discernible through the thick brown hair. (There was a fair amount of gray in the hair too, more than I remembered.) The blood seemed to have come mostly from the nose and mouth, an observation that had a surprising effect on my stomach. I hurried into the bathroom and threw up, feeling faint. When I felt better, I flushed the toilet, went back into the living room, gaze at eye-level and breathing through the mouth, and dialed the emergency number. I felt a wave of panic when the officious-sounding woman who answered asked my name, but I gave it.

"George Kilgore." Ex–forest ranger. Ex–resource officer, actually. Never made it to ranger. Presently working in horticulture and corpse-discovery. I wished I still worked for the Forest Service. The police might like another man-in-uniform. Instead, they'd wonder why I'd quit.

The officious woman told me to wait: they'd have someone with me directly. I wasn't feeling very patient. What do you do in that situation? Raid the icebox? Beer didn't appeal anymore. Blackwell probably wouldn't have much in his icebox except the odd herpetological specimen, frozen newt or dismembered frog. That thought impelled me to wait out on the sidewalk. I got there as a cruiser was pulling up. The two heavily armed women it contained were nervous, their eyes glancing off mine. One was black, the other Filipino or Guamanian. I couldn't think of anything to say, but after some more sidelong inspection, they saved me the trouble.

"Are you the person who called, sir?" The social distance a term of respect can establish in our disrespectful society is impressive. I felt as though they'd lowered a bell jar over me.

"Could you direct us to the problem, sir?" They clearly wanted *me* to go first up the shadowed walk to Blackwell's back-door entrance. I did, nerves tingling all over my dorsals. Inside, one looked at the body while the other looked at me. She kept looking at me as her partner phoned, told me that Detective Somebody would be there shortly, and then became very interested in my address, occupation, relationship to Blackwell, and immediate travel plans. Then we hung in silence over poor Blackwell for what seemed an excessively long time. I thought of asking them to cover him, but it seemed pointless.

Finally a plump little man skipped through the door, followed by a tall, morose one with a black carrying case. While the morose man rummaged in the case with his back to me, the plump man introduced himself politely as Detective Grunewald, shook

15

my hand, glanced at me the way a good-humored doctor might glance at a hypochondriac, and became absorbed in the police-woman's notebook.

"You're from Trinity County."

"Uh-huh."

"Beautiful place to live. My dad used to take me up there fishing. Good fishing. Bing Crosby used to go fishing up there."

"Not so good anymore."

"Mm. What brings you to the city?"

"I came to pick up a shipment of flats."

"Flats?"

"To plant tree seedlings in. Styrofoam flats."

"Ah. Says here you're a horticulturist. You plant trees?"

"Uh-huh."

"Why?"

"Why?"

"What for?"

"For replanting logged areas."

"What kind of trees?"

"Douglas fir and ponderosa pine. A little sugar pine. Alder and willow for creekbed restoration."

"You do this for money?"

"Yes."

"Who pays you?"

"Whoever wants them planted. Landowners. The Forest Service."

"You plant all these trees yourself? Sounds like a lotta work."

The morose man was setting up a tripod. None of the others seemed interested in our conversation, which for some reason made me feel more shy than if they had been listening avidly.

"I hire people to help."

"Sounds like a lotta work. You make any money?"

"Some."

"Ever plant any pot?"

"Excuse me?"

"Ever plant any dope? Marijuana?"

16

"Nope."

"Don't know why not. You could get rich up there from what I hear." The black policewoman glanced at the ceiling, unamused. Grunewald gave her the notebook and knelt beside Blackwell.

"We got another execution here. Who says capital punishment is cruel and unusual? Cruel it may be, but unusual it isn't."

"Capital punishment?"

"What did your friend do for a living, Mr. Kilgore?"

"He was a biologist. A herpetologist."

"One of those guys who collects snakes?"

"He worked mainly on amphibians."

"Frogs?"

"Salamanders, mainly."

"Salamanders?"

"They crawl instead of hop. Like lizards."

"I thought lizards were reptiles."

"They are."

"Are they valuable?"

"Lizards?"

"Salamanders."

"Valuable?" The policewoman glanced at the ceiling again. Grunewald was unperturbed.

"Are they worth a lot of money? Like parrots? Or cactuses?"

"Not that I know of."

"Hm. Well, your friend died like a smuggler, Mr. Kilgore. Somebody put a pistol to the back of his head. See the powder? It's a wonder the bullet didn't exit. Your friend must have had a lotta brains." The black policewoman shook her head. The other one sighed faintly and crossed her arms. Grunewald stood up and started wandering around the apartment, his voice drifting back to the living room. "When did you last see your friend?"

"We had dinner a couple of months ago."

"What does a herpetologist eat?"

"I think we had Japanese food."

"Raw fish?"

17

"Yes, as a matter of fact."

"It's good, isn't it? Sushi. Which do you like better? Squid or octopus?"

"Hm."

"I find squid a little strange raw, don't you?"

"Yes."

"It's good cooked, though. Did you get sick after you came in here?"

"Yes."

"You might have destoyed some evidence by flushing the toilet, did you know that?"

"Didn't occur to me."

"Pretty upsetting experience. Was your friend in good spirits when you had dinner?"

"Good enough."

"Meaning?"

"He wasn't that happy with his life."

"Why not?"

"He was divorced. Didn't like his job that much."

"Didn't like being a herpetologist?"

"Didn't like working at the Bayview Museum. He said there wasn't enough money for him to take collecting trips or to do research. He had to spend all his time giving talks to schoolchildren and doing paperwork."

"What paperwork does a herpetologist do?"

"Specimen catalogs. Environmental impact reports. Grant applications."

"How do you know?"

"He told me."

"So you talked about his problems. Did you talk about your problems?"

"Somewhat."

"What are your problems?"

"I'm divorced."

"And you don't like your job?"

"I like it pretty well. I quit the job I didn't like."

18

"Which was?"

"The Forest Service."

"Too much paperwork?"

"Among other things."

A medical-looking man arrived, and Grunewald went and huddled with him. The tall man took pictures, and more people kept arriving. Blackwell had never attracted so much official interest while he was alive, crouched in his cubicle at the museum. Or so much official money. The man-hours of the people in the apartment would have paid for a lot of field trips and research.

I began to feel like a wallflower, sitting on the couch with my hands folded while everybody else danced around Blackwell. I might have learned some forensic science from watching, but my mind was glazed. Eventually Grunewald noticed me again.

"You still here?" he said genially. "Go pick up your flats."

"I already did."

"Go have a drink then."

"Should I stay in town?"

"No, no. Go back to the woods and plant your trees. Just don't go to Colombia."

Chapter Two

I WANDERED OUT onto the street. The sun was getting low: I'd been in there a long time. My truck had been ticketed, which normally would have filled me with righteous indignation. Now I felt furtive. I hadn't been quite the open and impartial witness I'd tried to seem for Grunewald's benefit.

Blackwell and I had talked about more than jobs and marriages at the sushi bar. Grunewald's little trick question about growing dope had seemed alarmingly percipient, because that was precisely what I had been doing before I started the tree nursery. Blackwell and I had talked about growing dope, and we'd talked about smuggling cocaine. Two moonlighters comparing notes.

Or two not-very-successful middle-aged men bragging at each other. Blackwell and I had been friends for a long time, but we hadn't been communicating that much anymore. People's lives become accumulations of possessions and experiences, separate hilltops from which they shout back and forth at each other. It's not very conducive to mutual understanding. And Blackwell always had had a streak of exaggeration and fantasy: a strange thing in a scientist, I suppose, but then he wasn't quite making it as a scientist.

When we'd spent more time together, the exaggeration and fantasy had been a joy. Blackwell was one of those rare people who could make others share his fascination with himself. It's not that he was a solipsist: he was very interested in the world. But it was a very Blackwellian world, very filtered and slanted by his perceptions of it. I suppose that's why he could make it so interesting to others. Anyway, Blackwell could turn a walk to the corner grocery store to buy milk into an odyssey.

That had been when we'd spent more time together. When I was seeing him only a few times a year, when I was no longer involved in the adventures, the stories began to seem like a fog around him. Maybe it was just because I wasn't with him that much, but they began to seem unreal. It wasn't only that. The stories seemed to be changing, becoming less fanciful, more grandiose; duller and, at the same time, vaguer. When we were younger, a story about smuggling cocaine during an amphibian-collecting expedition to Central America would have been full of hair-raising escapes, grotesque ironies, colorful images. (Not that he'd been smuggling cocaine when we were younger. As far as I knew, it was a development of the past few years.) Now it sounded more like a news-magazine article on a profitable but risky financial venture, as though he was mining uranium. You had your capital and your technology and your markets, and it all came out on the bottom line. It was for money, not adventure.

Not that I had any right to criticize. I hadn't grown dope for any other reason, and I'd done it and talked about it just as colorlessly. Listening to Blackwell made me very uncomfortable for that reason. It made me recall how I'd bragged to him several years before, when I'd started making big dope money and he was a lowly assistant curator, last hired, with an estranged wife and a one-bedroom apartment in Oakland. I was afraid I'd given him ideas, though he'd never said any such thing, had never mentioned his sideline until the sushi bar. Then it had been like hearing a stranger talk. I'd lost any sense of his everyday life, and he hadn't filled me in. It almost seemed that he didn't have any, just venture capitalism.

Sometimes, halfway through some involved account, he would stop talking suddenly, and a confused look would come

21

over his face. He'd cough, take a bite of raw tuna or shrimp, then change the subject, or tell the rest of the story in a perfunctory, dispirited way. He'd lean back and sigh or look off to the side and seem very out of touch. I'd wondered how much of his product he was using.

How do you tell such things to the police? I wasn't really sure he *was* smuggling cocaine. I didn't know much about drug traffic outside my own little corner, and I didn't want to know about it. For me, the best thing about making money growing dope had been making *enough* to stop growing dope. Dope has been good to me, but I don't trust it. It's a tricky weed, *Cannabis*, an exotic opportunist that brings confusion and suspicion to whatever it touches (a good reason for legalizing it and taking it out of the hands of confused, suspicious people like me, but then are there any people who aren't that way?).

Trading marijuana is not unlike using it, euphoric and enriching under favorable circumstances, but undermined with deep troughs of panic and paranoia. I'd thought I'd crawled out of my last trough when I'd sold my third and last crop several years before, but Grunewald's trick question had made the floor of my world tremble and plunge. It was like being in a badly working elevator in a slowly burning building. The bottom didn't drop away completely, but holes opened up in it, and through them seeped fear. Of what, I'm not sure. Fear itself. An invisible, odorless substance in the air, like carbon monoxide, friendly little poison molecules eager to replace the hemoglobin in my blood and make me blue.

I waggled my shoulders and neck, trying to relax. I looked at the traffic. Driving north along the bay on I-80 is always beautiful. San Francisco is a fairy castle in the West with its towers and fogs and sailing ships. People complain about the high-rises, but the view from the east wasn't as fantastic before they built them. Still, driving north on that particular occasion, they did look a little too much like Disneyland, like the towers that Tinkerbell twinkled around, as though they existed mainly for the price of admission. It was just my frame of mind.

Chapter Three

I T WAS WELL PAST midnight when I got home, but Lewis was still up. Lewis is always up when I get home from a trip, and always upset. Lewis is a souvenir of my marriage, a big neu-tered tabby with a pathetically dependent attitude toward hu-mans and a ferociously hostile one toward other cats. Fortu-nately for Lewis, there aren't many other cats where I live (except for the odd bobcat or mountain lion, with whom Lewis does not interfere), since his hostility isn't matched by fighting prowess. Besides other cats, the main obstruction to Lewis's hap-piness is closed doors. He was upset because the door to my trailer had stayed closed while I was away.

Lewis has an interesting ritual for working out his feelings on this problem. First he runs up to me, making the most grating imaginable whining noises. When I go inside, he goes in too, but almost immediately demands to be let out, in the same grating tones. Then he demands to be let back in, scraping his claws across the screen door for emphasis. Then he demands to be let out again, and so on, for half a dozen or so times, until the door hinges have been thoroughly loosened.

Then Lewis is pleased. He celebrates. He sharpens his claws on the furniture and chases his tail. He demands to be let out again, and then he attacks the local trees. If he really is feeling megalomaniacal, he jumps from a tree onto my roof with a thud

23

that can wake me from a sound sleep. If I'm outside watching this feat (it is quite a jump), he looks down from the roof smugly, then starts making pitiful mewing sounds, as though he doesn't know how to get down again.

The ritual can get tedious, but Lewis has my sympathy in his neurosis. The door is his access to food and warmth, and he can open it only by scratching and complaining. What if it just stays closed someday? I believe Lewis worries about this. His sensitivity to my departures is so exquisite as to be mysterious and seems to belie a farsighted anxiety. One look at a suitcase and Lewis is gone. (He likes being taken on trips even less than he likes being left behind, irrational creature.) The invention of doors has had a major effect on the human psyche (try to imagine a doorless world), why not on the feline? I've thought of putting in one of those pet doors, but there are too many raccoons and skunks around, so Lewis has just had to cope, which he does pretty well, I suppose. From his viewpoint, if not from mine. I get tired of letting him in and out all the time.

I got tired of it quick on this occasion and gave Lewis a little kick to assist his third exit, which didn't stop him from demanding a fourth entrance. It may have dampened his enthusiasm a little, since he interrupted the ritual to have a bite of the food I'd set out in hope of distracting him. I had a glass of wine to counteract the coffee I'd drunk on the drive up, then ejected Lewis into the night. I heard him shredding tree bark as I got into bed.

I didn't have any bad dreams, but I woke up feeling as though I had. I woke up with a start, as though something had just caught up with me, as though Blackwell's ghost had taken an extra eight hours to get from Oakland to Trinity County. I hadn't dreamed about him, but he was there when I opened my eyes—right behind them, black stains and all. I drank some coffee and went outside. It was a nice morning, but then it's usually a nice morning in Trinity County in the summer.

I have ten acres beside the Trinity River. There used to be a town here in the gold-mining days, but about all that's left is a

24

big old barn that I've converted into a greenhouse of sorts for my seedlings. I moved the trailer here, which was depressing and embarrassing—formaldehyde insulation and all—but it was better than a tent. A mobile home in the woods: very contemporary.

It's a good place for growing things, although the soil isn't much, mostly river sand and gravel, if not plain rocks left from the mining. But there's plenty of sunlight and water. You have to make your own soil for growing tree seedlings anyway; it has to be just the right combination of humus, sand, and nutrients. I raise them from seed in the summer, then take them out and plant them in winter, which sounds simple but isn't. After several years of doing it, I'm still learning how complicated it is.

Natural functions usually seem mindlessly easy until you try to take them over. What could be simpler than the planting of a pine tree? The cone opens, the seed falls out, sinks into the duff, is flooded by melting snow, germinates. But when *I* want to plant a pine tree, it's another story. First I have to hire somebody to climb the trees and collect the ripe cones. Pine cones don't *drop* off the tree until the seeds are long gone. Then I have to run the cones through a contraption that separates seeds from cones, dry the seeds, fumigate them, prepare the soil, poke several seeds into each little hole in a styrofoam flat, thin the seedlings after they sprout, and keep them watered and shaded and fertilized through the summer.

Then I have to go back and plant the things all over again, in the ground. I have to get the seedlings out of the flats, pack them for safe transportation, hire a bunch of tree planters, get planters and trees to the woods, make sure the planters don't chuck the whole mess in the creek, and, once the seedlings are finally in the ground, attach a plastic guard to each so deer and rodents won't eat them. Sometimes, when I see a big old tree surrounded by natural-growth seedlings as thick as grass, I want to get down and crawl on all fours.

There's another little problem. Only trees can plant seeds mindlessly wherever they happen to be growing. If you're human, you have to plant them on somebody's property, and they have to pay you for it, or at least *say* they'll pay you. Some of my clients are waiting until the trees are full-grown before they pay me, just to make sure it's a sound investment—that's not quite fair. They're a sensible and understanding lot on the whole, the clients, but not rich. They're mostly owners of hill ranches who can see that the big cattle days are over (not that they ever were particularly big around here) and want to put up some hedges against a windy future. They have trouble enough meeting basic operating expenses, much less forking out for long-term investments like reforestation.

Growing dope had been easier than growing trees, to say the least, and considerably more lucrative. More lucrative than being a forester too, which is why I'd gotten into it. I suppose I became a forester for the wrong reasons. Growing up in the East, I had dreams of living in log guard stations and riding horses through mountain meadows, which would have been fine if I'd been growing up around 1908 when forest rangers did such things, guarding the forests from timber thieves, sheepmen, and poachers. I realized soon enough that forest rangers today spend most of their time driving pickups around logging roads, supervising timber sales and grazing allotments in a kind of mirror image of the romantic preservationism that had attracted me, but by then it was too late. I was in forestry school, telling myself I could be just like all the rest of the crew cuts, with their interest in stand density and board feet and their talk of pensions and home improvements.

Before I knew it, I was a resource officer in Trinity National Forest, with a house and a pregnant wife. There's only one way up in the Forest Service, by being transferred. They like to make sure a forester doesn't get too attached to a forest; otherwise he might not cooperate enthusiastically enough in cutting down all the trees in it. I was offered a promotion if I transferred to Daniel Boone National Forest in Kentucky, home of the dragline and the GEM (Giant Earth Mover). I told them I'd just as soon stay in the Trinity, thank you. They told me it was a free society and that they hoped I liked my resource officer's salary.

I'd gotten to know a few of the people who lived up the creeks: ladies in all-over tans and baggy denims and patchouli-and-sweat perfume; old men in ponytails and homemade leathers. My uniform seemed to attract them; maybe they felt nostalgic for authority, like vegetarians passing a hamburger stand. I'd seen some of their little sinsemilla patches and thought how easily one might have been harvested by somebody with a pickup and a knowledge of the roads. I'd quickly realized that this was a dangerous illusion, that even if a patch was not closely watched, selling pirated dope would not be pleasant. But I knew better growing places than the ones I saw, places where the water was closer and more plentiful, the angle of light better, the concealment of surrounding forest more complete.

I'm not going into detail; there are plenty of how-to books. Of course, I had an advantage. I was a corrupt official, using public land for private profit. Not that I felt very guilty. I felt anxious, but not guilty. Using public land for private profit is what the Forest Service is all about, or so it seemed to me. We bureaucrats mapped the forest, counted the trees, and put roads along every ridge and up every canyon so that private timber companies could cut and sell the trees at a profit. Recreation, wildlife, watershed, and all the other multiple-use holy log-rolling were frosting on the cake. I wasn't corrupting myself out of any cocoon of piny innocence. My innocence had been in joining the Forest Service thinking I could be a land steward instead of a timber warehouseman.

I moonlighted at dope farming for a couple of years, then quit the Service, sank all my capital into the venture, raised a bumper crop, hit the market just right, and came up with a hefty, untaxable profit. I knew I'd get stepped on if I tried to keep it up: modern capitalism does not love the lone entrepreneur. So I liquidated. I don't think I've ever known a more soul-satisfying pleasure than that which I felt in disposing of my dope operation. People usually come to hate the instruments of their liberation because of all the guilt or anxiety they associate with them. That's why revolutions end up liquidating revolutionaries.

I pulled out my ingenious system of plastic pipes and pumps and timers and trashed it like a pile of old boards, smashed it to bits and hauled it to the dump. I could have sold it to some hopeful, but I didn't want to leave any tracks. After trashing the technology, I took an equal delight in turning my little plantation back to the forest. I sowed it with rare native grasses and wildflowers, planted pine and oak seedlings, cleaned out the spring I'd developed, and planted sedge and azaleas around it. I didn't leave a piece of junk or a damaged plant on the site. It would take a genius archaeologist to figure out what I was up to there.

And here I am now, surrounded with plastic pipes, pumps, and timers for keeping my tree seedlings moist through the hot Trinity Canyon summer. Sometimes I wish I hadn't trashed the other stuff. I've spent a lot of my fortune putting this place together, and the money still goes out faster than it comes in. I'm not complaining. I'm legal, even respectable. People may know where the money came from, but they take it with a smile. I'm local business, an employer. It's a suspiciously ecological business, and my employees are hippies with nothing better to do in the winter, but it's a business.

I tell myself I should feel secure, but I don't. We grow up with the idea that making a lot of money is like getting married: you live happily ever after. Maybe it was like that once. But it goes so fast these days, even when you're not paying taxes on it. A bank account is like a leaky barrel. I was beginning to see the bottom of mine. Finding Blackwell was an unpleasant reminder of something I didn't like to think about: if I wanted to tear off a big lump of money again, I wasn't going to do it growing fir trees.

Throughout the day the thought dragged at my enthusiasm for planting fir trees. Sticking seeds into styrofoam holes may not seem like backbreaking work, but try doing it for eight hours. It's very worthy toil, of course. Reforest the land, create jobs, stop soil erosion, protect wildlife, conserve water, lah-de-dah. The piss-firs at the ranger station think I'm a dilettante. (Piss-fir is short for Piss-fir Willy, a term of endearment for Forest Service personnel hereabouts.) The hippies who work for me think I'm a mean old capitalist. *I* think I'm some kind of feeble-minded martyr.

Chapter Four

I WOKE UP with a stiff neck the next day. I wondered how stiff it would get after another decade or so of bending over seed flats. Lewis was scratching at the door. I let him in, and he sniffed at his bowl of cat chow, then went into the living room and sat down. I made some coffee and orange juice and started to fry an egg.

I glanced into the living room and saw Lewis disappearing into the bedroom, moving low on the floor the way he does when there's thunder over the mountains. I went in there to look out the window, wondering if there was a bear in the yard or something. I realized with a start that somebody was standing just outside the screen door. I couldn't see any features, only a shadowy form against the bright morning sunlight. I was still in my bathrobe.

"I guess I came too early," said the shadowy form. It was a nice, resonant voice with a whimsical edge. An attractive voice. I felt better.

"Depends on what you came for."

"The coffee smells good."

"Come in and have some." I opened the door. He was medium height with a ruddy face and black hair. He wore the usual denim and flannel, but there was something fine-grained about him that seemed a little foreign, to Trinity County at least. His hands might have been manicured at some time in the not-too-recent past. I'd never seen him anyway, and I've seen most of the people who live up here.

"Want some eggs?"

"No, thanks, but don't let me interrupt you."

I salvaged a well-cooked egg from the pan and sat down to eat it. He sat across from me, smiling, and sipped his coffee. This went on for several minutes, until I got a little nervous. I wondered if he'd been advised that it was considered rude to get down to business too quickly in the country, but he seemed too self-assured. He seemed the type who wouldn't care what people thought of him, country or city. Finally I broke the silence, feeling a little one-upped.

"What can I do for you, Mr.—?"

"Rice. Alec Rice."

"I'm George Kilgore."

"I know. I saw your ad in the paper."

"Ah."

"How do you like mobile-home living?" A salesman?

"Hm. I'm going to build a house, actually. When I get the time."

"Aren't you kind of close to the river here? Nice spot."

"It never floods since they built the dam."

"That's right."

"Never does much of anything. Just sits there in the silt."

"Nothing a lot of gelignite wouldn't fix."

"You must be a rafter."

"Actually, that's a little bit hearty for my taste."

"Beer commercials?"

"Precisely."

"Hey, that's a good word. I would have said 'exactly.'"

He smiled. I liked him. He looked pensive.

"Building houses costs money," he said.

"Exactly."

"I may be in the market for a large quantity of tree seedlings."

"I'm your man."

31

"You plant them as well as grow them?"

"That's right."

"Could you come out and look at my place today?"

"I don't know why not. Where is it?"

"South of Hayfork. Why don't you come with me right now?"

"I don't know why not." I went into the bedroom to dress. Lewis was crouching at the rear of the closet, pretending to be a shoe. I dragged him out with a great scratching of claws on the floor and put him outside, where he promptly disappeared under the porch. I realized that there was no vehicle out there.

"Where's your car?"

"I parked down the drive. Didn't want to stir up dogs or anything."

When I was ready, we started down the drive, which is screened by some oaks from State Highway 299.

"You found out about me from the paper?"

"Well, I heard about you too. I was here the other day, but you were gone."

We came to his car, which wasn't a car but a big two-seater pickup like the ones the timber companies use. That was a surprise. I'd thought Alec might have a hundred acres with a summer cabin on it and a Volvo station wagon. Even more of a surprise were the two large men in the front seat. The one on the passenger side looked Indian, with dark skin, button eyes, and glossy black hair. The one behind the wheel looked like a conquistador minus the helmet and cuirass: aquiline nose, sensual lips, curly bronze beard, pale blue eyes. A jumbo conquistador: his head would have touched the roof if he hadn't been leaning slightly forward to grip the wheel with forearms like legs of lamb. Both men glanced at me as I came alongside, but they didn't turn to say hello when I got in the back seat.

"Hi, I'm George Kilgore." Popular and genial forester. The Forest Service grooms you in public relations. There was an unenthusiastic pause.

32

"This is Rodrigo," said Alec, "and Jimmy." They turned their heads a little, first the conquistador, then the Indian. The conquistador, Rodrigo, started the truck and backed with great speed and finesse out the drive. We were in high gear, heading east toward Weaverville, before I could draw a breath. Alec and Jimmy took it in stride.

It was going to be another hot day, but the grass along the road was still pretty green. At about two thousand feet, the Trinity Canyon doesn't bake out as early in the hot season as the lower valleys, but it would get pretty dry later on. The river was still running high, as high as the dam would let it.

"See many salmon last winter?"

"Saw one in a sushi bar in San Francisco."

"Not here, though?"

"They don't spawn in silt. The river doesn't scour its bed enough since the dam stopped the floods."

"Too bad."

"You like to fish?"

"Oh, I used to. Too busy these days."

I thought of asking him what he did, but I didn't really want to look a gift horse in the mouth.

Alec gazed at the shrunken river. "They're so afraid of wasting resources that they end up wasting them."

I knew just what he meant. So afraid of letting a river's power and water go to waste that they end up wasting the river. Or the Forest Service: so afraid of losing a few board feet to fire or insects or environmentalists that they'll pile one timber sale on top of another until there's not a tree standing or a piece of soil for one to grow in.

Alec didn't say much after that as we sped through Weaverville, then over the river and through the clear-cut woods to Hayfork, then up into the tangle of hills drained by the Mad River and the Middle Fork of the Trinity. It's not real snow-capped wilderness like the Trinity Alps, but pretty remote. There are plenty of dirt roads and ranches, many dating back to

33

gold rush days, but the terrain is so rugged and heavily vegetated that it's still wild. You get the feeling that all kinds of unexpected things might live up there.

Alec's place certainly was a surprise. After we'd passed through a very sturdy locked gate, we drove for about a half hour before reaching his headquarters, and Rodrigo covered the road pretty fast, even over canyons and streambeds and windy ridgelines. I saw right away that Alec's offer to buy trees from me was legitimate. Somebody had done a thorough job of removing the ponderosa pine and Douglas fir that had been there, leaving a jungle of hardwoods and brush. I mentally began to lick my chops. There was enough to keep me going a long time, and Alec seemed the type who might pay bills, although I wondered about that a little when we finally pulled into the ranch compound. It looked like a typical, unprofitable hill operation: big old rickety barns, a pleasant but peeling and mildewed ranch house, plywood outbuildings, junk piles, wandering chickens. Alec and I got out on the dusty patch of earth in the middle of all this, and he said something in Spanish to Rodrigo, who pulled the truck out of sight behind a barn.

"You can see the whole property from that knoll," Alec said, pointing at a rocky hilltop that still had some big firs on it. "We'll take a walk up there, then come back here and talk. Wendy! Hey, Wendy!" He looked toward the ranch house, and I saw that there was a woman lying on a chaise lounge beside it, wearing a string bikini. She had one of the most beautiful bodies I've ever seen. She didn't say anything.

"Fix us some lunch in about an hour, okay?" Wendy still didn't say anything, but Alec seemed satisfied. He strode off toward the hilltop. I had to hurry to keep up, but I got a quick glance into one of the barns, expecting to see decrepit tractors. Another surprise: it was piled to the top with glass and aluminum, which, as a horticulturist, I recognized. Greenhouse parts.

Alec was one of those people who do everything with full concentration. He didn't say a word as he climbed to the hilltop. When we got there, he talked a very great deal, indeed. He knew

34

everything there was to know about his great big ranch: which landmarks indicated the borders, what the watersheds were, how many board feet had been logged out by the previous owner, how many head of stock had been run on it, how much soil erosion and stream siltation there was.

"They took this place to the cleaners," he said, "but I'm not going to. Couldn't if I wanted, it's pretty much wrung out. I'm not going to carve it into eighty-acre ranchettes, either. I'm not even going to run cattle on it. I'm going to make a sustained-yield forest out of it."

"Nice work if you can get it," I said, but not out loud.

"We don't really understand about forests in this country," Alec continued. "We're too fat. We think we can get something for nothing, and a little extra after that: logs and meat and happy fun too. The Old World, they understand about forests. The Chinese, the Germans. If you're going to have a forest, you damn well have a forest, and none of this crap about multiple use. Anybody that grazed their sheep in *those* forests got the chop."

If Alec wanted to decapitate any shepherds who got their flocks into my plantings, it was okay with me. I did wonder a little about his choice of nationalities. Chinese was fine, very whole earth and new age, but German? I stole a glance at his footwear. They looked like L. L. Bean moccasins: definitely not jackboots. Not even cowboy boots.

"You might be able to make a living off an operation of this size once you got it going," I said, getting into the can-do spirit. The idea didn't seem to excite him particularly.

"Forestry in this country is about where the Germans were fifty years ago. Clear-cuts and even-aged stands. The Germans gave that up. They're much more into diversity now."

"I could plant some sugar pine along with the ponderosa and Douglas fir. There's getting to be a market for hardwoods too. Black oak. Might even be close enough to the coast for tan oak and golden chinquapin."

Alec looked me in the eye, which wouldn't have been unusual in a serious business discussion except that he kept doing it after other people would have stopped. He had blue eyes, not very expressive ones. I didn't know what he was trying to do, challenge me or gaze into my soul or what. It got embarrassing, so that I finally broke the contact by casting my eyes appraisingly toward the pine stumps on the slopes below us, as though calculating how many new trees I would make grow there. He started talking again.

"It takes a lot of strength and discipline to grow forests. Much more than it takes to cut them. Americans like their macho fantasies, but they're flabby compared to the Old World. They've had it easy for two hundred years, but it's going to get a lot tougher a lot faster."

I realized that I was unconsciously straightening my spine. Strength and discipline. I sat on a stump. Clients have their little individualities.

"You think you could grow a forest here?" said Alec.

"How's your deer population?"

"I've heard you have some initiative. You seem a little different from most of these time-servers."

Ah, yes, the pension. How I've yearned for my lost pension at times. I remember talking to one of the old-timey foresters who came in from the CCC in the thirties. He went on for a half hour about the mindless, faceless, technobureaucratic green machine, then sighed, "Oh well, only a year to my pension."

Alec regained my wandering attention by suggesting we go back for lunch. We passed Jimmy and Rodrigo, who were doing something with a very large, new piece of earth-moving equipment. I couldn't resist asking this time.

"You must have, uh, other sources of income."

"Oh, yeah."

Wendy had a fairly lavish lunch waiting for us on our return, somewhat to my surprise. She didn't share it with us. She served us, still wearing the string bikini, then went back outside.

Wanting to seem disciplined and strong, I began talking about labor costs and plantings per acre as we ate, but Alec got a little vague. I offered to come back with detailed plans right away, and he said he'd appreciate that but that he was sure I had other commitments and there was no hurry. I certainly didn't want to tell him I had no other commitments (I had commitments, but no apparent golden geese like Alec), so I subsided. Wendy had produced some delicious white wine into which it was very easy to subside. Alec knew all about wine, as he seemed to know all about everything else. I wondered a little why he was wasting such a nice wine on me—it was like giving it to the plumber or the washing machine repairman, after all. But I didn't wonder too hard. I'm a likable guy.

I was in a golden haze by the time Alec had Jimmy drive me home. As I got into the truck, I took a last look at Wendy, who was lying on her stomach now, the strings untied, with a tall glass beside her. In the dimness of the house, I hadn't noticed that she had a large yellow bruise on the back of one of her shapely thighs.

"Talks a blue streak, don't he?" said Jimmy, about forty-five minutes later as we pulled into Hayfork Valley. I looked up in surprise. The haze was wearing off.

"You speak English."

"Sure, man, I speak English."

"Sorry, I thought because he spoke Spanish to you—."

"Rodrigo doesn't speak it."

"You're Mexican?"

"Guatemalan."

"How'd you come to work for Alec?"

"A job's a job." With that I could agree.

Chapter Five

I HAD A HEADACHE by the time Jimmy dropped me. The phone was ringing, and I docilely rushed to answer it, tripping over Lewis on the porch. The trailer was like an oven, but what can you expect when you live in a metal box? I turned on the air conditioning and picked up the evilly jangling telephone. It was Detective Grunewald.

"I want to talk to you. Can you come down here tomorrow?" It wasn't exactly a question. He didn't seem to like me anymore. "There are some things I want to ask you about." Uh-oh.

"Gee, I'm kind of busy right now."

"We'd appreciate it if you could help us out."

"Could we just talk on the phone?"

"There are some things I'd like you to look at."

"Gas is so expensive."

"Yeah, too much for our budget. So we'd appreciate your help. As a citizen."

I spent a restless night. Drinking in the daytime gives me insomnia. I had plenty to think about. Alec Rice was evidently some kind of dope mogul (greenhouses were the coming thing) and maybe a little unhinged. But so what? Why not grow trees for somebody with money for a change? I didn't have any ethical prejudices against dope growing, just psychiatric ones. If I was as heavily invested in dope as Alec appeared to be, I'd probably have a slight Napoleon complex too. Occupational hazard. Still, there was something a little ominous about his popping up just then, almost like another ghost from my extra-legal past. And then there was Grunewald's inconsiderate tone. What had moved him to be so disagreeable? A phone call to the Trinity County sheriff's office, which long had admired me from afar? They had looked but not touched, but I was afraid they remembered.

It was a pretty drive next morning. There was still plenty of whipped-cream snow on the Trinitys and on Shasta and Lassen. The conifers showed purple and yellow tints with their new cones, and the hardwood leaves were still bright green, just beginning to toughen and darken for the long summer. Of course, the edges of the postcard were a little smeared and frayed by the hydraulic mining spoil, the old clear-cuts, the silted spawning beds, and the red mud bathtub ring around Whiskeytown Reservoir. Things got even blotchier after I dropped out of the mountains, first through the sprawl of Redding, then through the rice paddies and the forsaken eucalyptus groves of the Sacramento Valley, buzzing with cropdusters at this time of year, and finally past the new tracts that cling so nakedly to the steep rangeland between Davis and Richmond.

There's nothing quite as naked as California urban sprawl. It sits on the dry hills like an overdone roast, land as butcher's meat, processed and consumed. No frills or garnishes, no genteel overlay of summer greenery or winter snow as in the East. There's a kind of purity to it. Things always have been right out in the open in California, from the old Mexican days when they stripped the hides from the cattle and left the carcasses for the condors and grizzlies, when they ran so much stock on the hills that they turned black with starved and rotting cows in the drought years.

Grunewald nodded at me when I finally reached his cubicle in the Oakland police department's building. He didn't stand up to shake hands, but he did offer me a seat. He pushed some photographs across the desk.

39

"From the autopsy." I recognized the back of Blackwell's head, but not much else. Talk about butcher's meat. "The bullet punched out a kind of plug of bone from the back of his skull as it entered. Slowed it down, which is why it didn't exit. I wish they all could be so neat. Actual death was by suffocation from all the blood that ran into his lungs, but he probably lost consciousness immediately. May not have been too conscious before anyway."

"What do you mean?"

"Gallbladder was rich in alkaloids. He was all doped up. Probably cocaine."

Grunewald showed me some newspapers. "Oakland Biologist Shot in Home." "Execution-style Slaying." "No Suspects at This Time." It hadn't made the front page. There were no followups.

"Too bad your friend didn't get killed in Trinity County," Grunewald said. "We get a murder a day down here. He was lucky to get autopsied so fast. We got basements full of bodies."

"Why was he—lucky?"

"Never know what you might turn up in one of these execution-style killings."

"Turn up anything?" Studied casualness.

"Not much." Grunewald gave me a look of bored dislike. "Your friend was an active user, and you're an inactive grower."

"Excuse me?"

"I talked to your sheriff's department. You're kind of well known up there, you know? But they said I could have you if I wanted."

"What?"

"Don't bat your eyes at me, surfer boy." Being tall, blond, and blue-eyed is not always an advantage in these troubled times. Grunewald grunted and emptied an envelope on the desk. It didn't look promising: some scraps of charred paper. "Lucky your friend had a nice ecological wood stove." He spread out the scraps. "Mean anything to you?"

There were scraps of green paper with irregular black and red lines, of white paper with blue lines, of beige and pink paper with black lines.

"Looks like pieces of maps and notebooks. Probably from his biological work. Maybe some pieces of publications, environmental literature."

"Why maps?"

"For collecting trips. Collecting herpetological specimens."

"His boss at the museum thought so too. Recognize any words?"

"Words?"

"See? There's handwriting on some of these."

" 'de'? 'stal gr'? 'ew'? 'xter'? 'cyan'? Doesn't ring any bells."

"I thought you knew this natural history stuff. 'Stal gr' could be 'costal grooves'. That's a word for describing salamanders. 'Cyan' could be a Greek word for 'blue' that they use in scientific descriptions."

"So what was Blackwell's boss's theory?"

"He didn't have one. He said Blackwell seemed depressed. There wasn't much for him to do at the museum since their budget got cut. He thought maybe Blackwell's job would be axed if it got cut again this year."

"Doesn't seem like a reason for murder."

"Seems like a reason for Blackwell to look for other sources of income. Looking a little too hard, maybe?"

I shrugged. Grunewald leaned back in his chair and clasped his hands behind his head.

"You knew he was smuggling cocaine, didn't you? Trips to Central America?"

"What if I did?"

"It raises some possibilities. You could be withholding evidence. That makes you an accessory."

"I haven't seen him since the dinner I told you about."

"You expect me to believe you now?"

"I don't have to talk to you."

"No, you don't. You could spend the next couple days in jail

41

and not talk to anybody except a lawyer. Not that I want you. I don't like you druggies. You don't pay taxes."

"That's not our fault."

"Life is not fair." He snatched up the envelope and started stuffing the scraps back in, not very carefully. I had thought evidence was handled with kid gloves. He moved his chair around to a filing cabinet; put envelope, photos, and clippings in it; and slammed it shut. "Ah, get out of here, Kilgore."

"Who do you think killed him?"

"I should tell you?"

"You have suspects, then?"

"You'll be the first to know, okay?" He picked up the phone and started dialing. It seemed like an awfully short conversation for such a long drive, but I didn't say so.

Chapter Six

I STOOD OUTSIDE the building, feeling reluctant to get in the truck and drive another five hours back to Trinity County. The Bayview Museum was nearby. I put some more change in my parking meter and drifted in that direction, past joggers and sea gulls and winos. It was getting on toward rush hour anyway, a bad time to be on the freeway.

Blackwell hadn't told me he was about to *lose* his job, only that he was sick of it. It was the kind of thing he wouldn't have minded telling me ten years before. Failure gets more shameful the older you get, which is logical enough. The young have more time to try again. Failure had been a kind of joke to Blackwell and me when we'd been in school together. There'd been plenty of failures to share: not getting top grades, not getting some girl, not getting on the list of "mosts" in the yearbook. There'd been a kind of solidarity in failure then, surrounded by all the discontented successes of a fairly well-to-do suburb.

It was less amusing after that. They called the post–World War I generation the "lost" generation and the post–World War II generation the "beat" generation. They should call the post-Vietnam generation the "closing door" generation. When we were in high school, there was a television commercial that had us all shaking in our boots. It showed an eager young scholar in a mortarboard clutching a high school diploma and standing outside a wrought-iron gate. The scholar smiles confidently, but then an ominous chord is struck, and a solemn voice explains that there are many more scholars than there are places for them in college. The gate swings shut, leaving the crestfallen scholar outside.

Not that we were kept out of college. I went to State and Blackwell went to some self-congratulating little men's college. The "closing college door" was just one of society's little tricks for keeping us in line, there being no surer way of making people line up for something than telling them they probably can't have it. But as we went along, another door always seemed to be closing, or threatening to close, just ahead of us, some door to opportunity or privilege that we were just a little too late, in our baby-boom millions, to get through.

After the closing college door, it was the closing job door. There weren't enough jobs for Forestry M.S.'s or Herpetology Ph.D.'s: too many hopeful young foresters and biologists. When we finally got them, it was after more years than we liked to count of seasonal employment and temporary grants and just plain coolie labor. Then it was the closing advancement door. We were just a little old by then to be starting to climb ladders, and the rungs on which we found ourselves were not particularly advantageous ones. We never made it through that door. I suppose you could say we learned the true meaning of the term *drop out*. Dropping out is supposed to be kind of lazy and benign and relaxed. For us, it was more like stepping unwarily into an empty elevator shaft.

We had some good years—when I was new in the Trinity and Blackwell was new at the Bayview. Everything was new then: new jobs, new wives, new cars, new state. To have a job in California: that was something, even if the jobs weren't quite what we dreamed of when wandering around the town reservoir, looking for wood turtles, me dreaming of log cabins and Blackwell dreaming of expeditions to find flying frogs and leaping lizards. Blackwell learned from a mutual high school acquaintance that I worked in the Trinity and dropped in during one of the

collecting trips he'd often taken before Proposition 13. Hobnob-
bing with a research biologist varied my bland diet of piss-fir
talk. We traded inside information a lot, though it didn't seem
to do us much good.

We had a kind of exclusive club for a while: Blackwell and
his wife, Joan; Diane and I. We tasted glossy pleasures: ski trips,
Baja, hot springs, a little high-class dope. We felt, perhaps
looked, like golden youth. The pleasures were a little rich for our
salaries, though. We were speculating on our shiny new jobs.
You might say we'd lost our faith in failure. We'd come to expect
promotions and raises or, at least, better jobs somewhere else.
When that didn't happen, things fell apart.

They fell apart for me anyway. I didn't really know what had
happened to Blackwell. As I walked along the stone facade of
the museum, I realized that I wanted to know. I didn't know *why*
I wanted to know. It wasn't really because I was afraid of being
a suspect. Grunewald wouldn't have been so casual and nasty if
he'd suspected me. I wasn't feeling vengeful either; as I said,
Blackwell could have been run over by a truck. His death was
his business. But—I suppose I was curious. I'm always curious
about what's happened to people I've known. People drop out
of sight so completely that they might as well be dead. Usually
my curiosity is dulled by a fear of finding out what *did* happen
to them. They might have done so well that I'll feel ashamed, or
so badly that I'll feel frightened and depressed. But Blackwell's
fate already had frightened and depressed me. I figured I might
at least have the satisfaction of *understanding* it.

I skirted a flock of schoolchildren and entered the lobby of the
Bayview. Tranquillity descended upon me; I like museums.
There's nothing like a quiet afternoon in a museum, with the
dust motes lazily swirling in the sunbeams from the skylights. I
drifted into the natural history section for a glance at my favorite
dioramas. I know stuffed animals are supposed to be macabre,
but I find them less so than zoo animals. Stanley, the explorer,
once said that for every slave delivered to the coast of Africa, a
large family had been killed. The same has been true of zoo ani-

mals for most of the time there've been zoos. A stuffed skin in a museum represents one death: how many does a live captive represent?

I looked at a mountain lion reclining on a ledge above a rolling vista of sun-baked hills, with two ravens scolding him from the cliff face. There was still a kind of mystery about those bundles of dry fur and feathers. Dead things and wild things have one thing in common: their prospects are unknown to us. Everybody knows what the prospects of zoo animals are: lunch and then dinner.

There are a lot more zoos than museums. People don't really like unknown prospects. Zoos are more labor intensive too, and we cling to whatever keeps us busy. I didn't stay long with my quiet friends in the dioramas. I sidled up to a gray door marked "Staff" and slipped inside. It wasn't a scene of bustling activity, the staff section; in fact, it was deserted except for a volunteer receptionist and Dr. Todd, Blackwell's boss. He seemed glad to talk to somebody about his deceased assistant curator.

"It's unbelievable," he said, "what happens to people these days." He was a pleasant-looking man in tortoiseshell glasses, one of those people who could be any age from thirty-five to fifty-five. He had a fair-size office, unlike the cinderblock cubicles of his absent staff; but it was piled so high with scientific journals, environmental impact reports, and other unlovely paperwork that the effect wasn't affluent. "You were the friend who found him?"

"Yes."

"They have no idea who did it?"

"Not that I know of."

"Do they even care that much? The detective I talked to was—brusque."

"Overworked, probably."

"Ah." Dr. Todd glanced at the mound of papers on his conference table. "I'm afraid I wasn't much help to them. Tom was sort of—disengaging from this institution. There wasn't much for him to do lately. We're kind of hanging on by our fingernails."

46

"Do you have any idea what he was doing outside of work?"

"He was taking field trips. Some to your part of the country, I think."

"Recently? He didn't tell me he'd been up there."

"Tom wasn't telling anybody much recently. But I remember him calling one day when he was supposed to be here for a meeting. His car had broken down. I think he said he was in Siskiyou County."

"Did you ask what he was doing up there?"

"Not under the circumstances."

"You were getting ready to fire him?"

Todd leaned back in his chair and raised his voice a little. "No, I wasn't getting ready to fire him. The city council might have been getting ready to fire him. I'd be hiring people if I had any money to pay them. They think a museum's finished because it's filled with exhibits. A pile of labeled specimens. We don't have names for a lot of the invertebrates in this state, and we know next to nothing about the ones we *have* named."

"You weren't paying for his field trips?"

"Unfortunately not."

"Did he keep notes from them in his office here?"

"I really couldn't say."

"Could I look through his office?" Dr. Todd looked uncomfortable.

"I think the police investigated it pretty thoroughly."

"Did they take the stuff away?"

"No. In fact, I've been wondering what to do with it. I've never had a staff member murdered before. We asked about the funeral, but they said it was back east, where the relatives are. I guess I'll have to ask them to come and take it away or let us dispose of it. Do you know if he left a will or anything?"

"No. I'd like to know what happened to him. You could watch me while I looked."

"You were a good friend of his?"

"Yes."

"I don't suppose it would do any harm." Dr. Todd brushed

47

aside a two-volume copy of the *California Desert Plan* that blocked his exit from behind his desk, sidled past a coffee-table-shaped raft of papers on the carpet, and led me down the hall to one of the cubicles. "It's half an office, actually. He doubled up with our geologist."

The cubicle looked a little eerie, like one of those anatomical dummies that show half a body covered with skin and hair, the other pared to muscle and bone. The geologist's half was littered with snapshots, diagrams, maps, greeting cards, bookshelves, and the usual piles of paperwork. Blackwell's was gray desktop and cinderblock and carpet. Todd seemed surprised.

"Now wait just a minute." He stepped out of the office abruptly and hurried off down the hall. I stuck my head out and heard him talking rather heatedly to the receptionist. I turned back to the empty desk. I opened one of the drawers idly, opened it all the way, and saw a single paper stuck behind it. I'm always losing papers that way. I pulled it out, tearing it in the process. I could hear Todd coming back along the hall. I stuffed the paper in my pocket and quietly closed the drawer. Todd seemed a little shaken.

"Some men came and took it all away at lunchtime. These volunteers! She didn't even ask who they were. 'They seemed to know what they were doing'!"

"I suppose it was just the usual kind of stuff. Books and papers."

"I suppose so. They ought to cremate us with our paperwork. Save on fuel."

I left Dr. Todd on the phone, trying to get through to some authority on the matter of Blackwell's disappearing effects. I waited until I was back in my pickup to take the paper out of my pocket. Getting furtive. It was cheap, beige paper with a photograph of some big Douglas firs blurrily reproduced at the top. "Save Limestone Canyon," it said.

I knew about Limestone Canyon. It was one of the thousands of environmental issues that never make the bigtime, so to speak, that never quite become causes célèbres, but limp from hearing to hearing without enough people getting interested in them, pro or con, for much to happen. The Middle Bar Ranch Corporation in Siskiyou County had been trying to dam Limestone Canyon for fifteen years—every time its boy-wonder owner, Pierre Grenville, got in an expansive mood. The Middle Bar owned about two-thirds of the canyon, one of the many private inholdings which our benevolent government tolerates in national forests. That the other third of the canyon was within the proposed boundaries of the Salmon Trinity Alps wilderness evidently didn't bother Grenville, but it did bother other people: enough to put a drag on his expansiveness, though not enough to get the government to buy the inholding. But Grenville was persistent, like one of those pegboard children's toys. They'd hammer him flat on one dam project, and he'd pop up with another one.

Before the Arab oil embargo, the dam had been to provide a recreational lake for a second-home community. Then, after a few dormant years, it resurfaced as a hydro-electric project. Two years later, during the drought, it was to be a water-storage facility. The fact that nobody much needed water storage in the vicinity didn't bother Grenville, but local environmentalists began to mutter about unholy alliances between the Middle Bar and Southern California developers, with Grenville's lake as a foot in the door for an impoundment system on the Klamath, Scott, and Salmon rivers that would make the Tennessee Valley look like a national park.

The trouble with Limestone Canyon was that it wasn't quite special enough. It had old-growth Douglas fir and broadleaf evergreen forest and good salmon and steelhead runs, but there were other canyons like that—fewer all the time—but still more than one, and several of them were fully within the national forest and thus easier to protect. I'd never even been in Limestone Canyon. Apart from the fact that foresters don't have much time for hiking (Limestone Canyon was roadless, as virtually all virgin canyons must be), it hadn't seemed worthwhile getting to know a place that could be underwater whenever Grenville got really resourceful and efficient. I'd heard about it from surveyors, who'd said it had some nice outcroppings and pools.

The paper was printed by the Limestone Canyon Defense Council. I knew some of the members: a harried assemblage of old and new residents—ranchers, packers, a few businessmen and professionals, new-age types, retirees, teachers. Nice people, but, like the place they were trying to protect, not quite notice-able enough to make headlines, and, thus, given the Forest Ser-vice's utter devotion to publicity and politics, cheerfully ignored.

It wasn't a very intriguing clue. In fact, it was boring. Anybody with a finger in environmental pies, as Blackwell was, would be sure to have piles of such things everyplace: home, office, car. Grunewald's charred scraps showed that. It was true that somebody had taken the trouble to burn Blackwell's papers, maybe to sneak into his office and steal some, but that didn't mean Limestone Canyon had anything to do with it. I stuffed the sheet into my glove compartment and drove over to Berkeley to get something to eat. Not sushi this time; I was off sushi.

Chapter Seven

I GOT HOME even later than I had the last time, but Lewis was up, avowing starvation. The large bowlful of cat food I'd left on the porch was gone, but raccoons might have eaten it. Lewis was never a fan of dry cat food, not that I blame him. Imagine a life spent gnawing on the textured vegetable protein they sell in backpacking stores. I gave him a bowl of milk.

I slept until noon, and the place was like an oven when I awoke. It gets cool at night here, but the temperature can shoot up to the nineties by midday. I put on my bathing suit and stumbled down to the river. On my way back I stopped by the garden. I hadn't seen it for several days, but it looked all right, a little wilted possibly. I turned the sprinkler on. It wasn't the greatest garden in the world. As I've said, Trinity Canyon soil leaves much to be desired, so a lot of composting is required, which is all right with me. I like making compost better than growing vegetables. It's less picky-picky. I get enough picky-picky with pine seedlings.

Diane had been the gardener of our ménage. She'd had infinite patience with a bewildering variety of flowers, vegetables, and fruits, from seed to harvest. I can deal with three or four types of plants from seed to harvest, but not with fifty. I suppose that's how agriculture got started: Men couldn't deal with the complexity of this gardening business that women had invented, so they started growing crops. I like to pump my energy into something big and showy, a cash crop, not into a hundred little things.

My garden made me sad actually, another reason for neglecting it. I may not like doing gardens, but I like having them. Looking at my poor attempts reminded me of what I'd had with Diane at our house in Weaverville.

Lewis was sitting beside the raspberry bed, looking enigmatic. Diane and I had hoped he'd become a gopher killer, but if he was he was very discreet about it. He'd stalk burrows sometimes, and occasionally a dead gopher would appear in the yard but never in direct association with Lewis. Cats usually are eager to show off their victims, and I wondered why Lewis seemed not to be. Afraid I'd feed him less if I knew he caught his own?

I picked some lettuce and peas. Vegetables do have their moments, and fresh peas are among the best, particularly after what you have to go through to get them—beds, frames, picking, shelling. All that greenery for a handful of peas, but they do taste wonderful, like a distillation of two thousand hours of sprouting, twining, flowering and so on. Eating becomes poetic, or seemed so as I ate the peas that evening, watching the sun go down. They might have tasted even better if there'd been someone around to appreciate my poetic pea perceptions. I wondered if Blackwell had had anybody like that recently. He hadn't told me if so.

There had been a certain parallelism about our marriages or, at least, about the disintegration of them. Whatever their individualities, marriages seem to disintegrate similarly. Diane and Joan were very different. Joan was small, dark, and aggressive; Diane was tall and blond. I wouldn't call her passive: she had her ways of getting what she wanted, but they were less direct than Joan's. They both wanted more or less the same things: space, options, hope, status—what everybody wants.

As I said, we had a good time for a while, but then things began to get thin. Joan got tired of working as a typist while Blackwell ran around on field trips, so she began running around with a television producer and eventually moved to Los Angeles. Diane got tired of working as a waitress, but her options in Trinity County were narrower than Joan's in the Bay Area. She decided to have a baby: she was good with growing things. I thought it was a good idea at the time. The transfer to Daniel Boone National Forest hadn't come up yet, and I still thought I had a career with the Forest Service.

They offered me the transfer in Diane's fifth month. She didn't mind the idea of it as much as I did. She had family in Illinois. She didn't like the idea of continuing forever on my resource officer's salary, which was one of the reasons I started eyeing sinsemilla patches. There's a synergy to these things once they get going. Diane got increasingly busy and distracted, first with being swollen up, then with the baby. It was a nice baby, blond hair, blue eyes. Mendel was right. There wasn't that much for me to *do* about a baby, though, except go out and make money to pay the bills. I went out and grew dope.

It didn't make things easier. You pay a price for feeding on both sides of the socioeconomic trough. People sense it when you've grown a second face. Maybe that's paranoia: nobody accused me of anything; they just glanced at me sidelong or stopped talking when I came into an office. Even the hippies became guarded. Worst of all, that kind of moonlighting is incredibly time-consuming. I must have been extremely lucky. I couldn't guard the crop twenty-four hours a day, but nobody stole it, either because they really didn't know where it was or they feared some kind of setup.

I was never home: the epitaph of a hundred million marriages. Diane knew what I was up to and didn't like it particularly but didn't want the responsibility of stopping me. She wouldn't have minded a little extra money. She lacked faith, though. She didn't believe I'd make any. She started visiting her parents in Illinois. First it was two weeks, then a month, then a summer. Three months is a long time these days. You can grow a whole new personality in three months. I had "changed" when Diane got back from that trip. Maybe I had. She moved in with a single woman friend, and I put the house on the market.

53

My hostility is showing. You just can't escape it in the wonderful world of divorce. Well, that was Diane's crime against me: lack of faith. It seemed justified at the time. The inflated real estate market was sagging, the house seemed unsalable, and I *hadn't* made a profit on my first two years of dope growing. I'd plowed it all back into the operation. I was still working for the Service then, getting bad evaluations for neglecting my duties.

My crime against Diane was a more literal one, actually illegal perhaps, fraud or something. Every time I think about it, the justifications start crowding into my head: Diane had left me, it was all my work, I needed the money, her father was putting her through a computer course in Illinois. I still feel like a criminal, almost like a murderer, as though I've killed Diane. She might as well be dead as far as my life is concerned, even though she doesn't know what I did to her. (I hope she doesn't. If she knew and did nothing, I'd really feel evil.)

What I did, of course, was keep all the profits for myself from my very successful third year. Oh, I pay very substantial child support, and I gave Diane more than her share of the house payments when I sold it, but she didn't get 50 percent of what I had when the divorce came through. Nowhere near 50 percent. Was that really so bad? The money's mostly gone. Diane has a good job now from what I hear. No permanent damage. Just a little temporary dishonesty, pettiness, selfishness, and meanness.

I always feel like I'm living at the bottom of a well when I think these thoughts. I contemplated the telephone. Calling Diane was not an option. There had been women since, but I didn't have anything very heartwarming to say to any of them. I wondered what Blackwell's ex-wife was doing. I wondered if Joan knew what had happened to him. I wondered if she might know why it had happened.

After some wandering around southern California directory assistance, I came up with a J. Blackwell in Santa Monica. I had no way of knowing if Joan had kept her married name, but some women do it, and I had no other options. The number was busy at first, then there was no answer. Around 11:30 I got a voice. It didn't sound like her, but it didn't sound like anyone else either.

"George *Kilgore?*" It was Joan. She always had affected a certain incredulity at my existence. A *forest ranger?* It occurred to me that her surprise at my calling might mean that she didn't know what had happened to Blackwell. I asked her. She hadn't. I told her. Silence.

"Joan?"

"Wait a minute. Goddamn it." It sounded as though she put the phone down. I waited. Her voice was different when she came back on the line. "I'm sorry, George; this comes at a bad time for me." I heard her blowing her nose.

"Maybe I shouldn't have told you like this."

"Oh, I don't know why not. Everything else is happening today. Where are you?"

"Trinity County."

"Still a forest ranger?"

"No, I'm self-employed now."

"Like it better?"

"Some. How are you doing?"

"I thought I was doing pretty well until last week, George, but I may have to get back to you on that."

"It's a bad time to talk."

"You're not interrupting anything."

"Joan, did you know that Tom was smuggling cocaine?"

"No, I didn't know that, George. I haven't talked to Tom in over a year. But I bet I know who could tell you about it." That was quick.

"Who's that?"

"His girlfriend."

"He had a girlfriend?"

"Didn't he tell you? Tom had a girlfriend about half the time we were married. He met her when we were in Eugene. She was one of his students when he was a teaching assistant. They used to go on field trips together."

"All the way back then?"

"All the way back then, George. Why did you think I left?"

"You think he was smuggling cocaine with her?"

"I don't know, George. What do you think?" The subject wasn't amusing her.

"Would he have gone on trips to Central America with her?"

"I don't know why not. He went every other damned place with her."

"What's her name?"

"Carla Shreve."

"Do you have any idea where she is now or how I might get in touch with her?"

"Be real, George."

"Oh, well, er—."

"How's Diane?"

"Pretty good from what I hear."

"How's the little girl?"

"Not so little anymore."

"Well, keep in touch."

"Yeah. Sorry."

Chapter Eight

I HAD TROUBLE with my water lines the next few days. You can't let tree seedlings go without water: they curl right up. I don't know how they survive in the wild around here, where almost half the year is dry. Sometimes after a heavy rain in late summer, the ground suddenly will be covered with thousands of pine and fir seedlings. I guess they survive by opportunism, like everything else.

But they won't be opportunists for *me*, the little devils. For me, they're all helpless and passive. Water us or else. So I pulled apart the plastic pipes to my spring and cleaned them out and stuck them back together. Things seemed to work better, not perfectly, but better. Then I went back to planting seeds. After spending a couple of days fiddling with a water system, you want to have something to water.

I was glad of the diversion actually. Finding out about Blackwell's girlfriend had set back my curiosity. I wasn't quite sure I wanted to know more after all. I'd like to say that this was because of moral fastidiousness. *I* hadn't had a girlfriend. I'm afraid it was more out of jealousy. *I* hadn't had a girlfriend. It wasn't just concupiscence: it was the discovery that Blackwell had possessed a realm of experience unknown to me, had gotten away with an extra piece of life, so to speak. Greedy greedy. It seemed a more pleasurable and interesting betrayal of spouse than mine had been. Maybe it was more justified. Maybe this Carla person was worth cheating for.

It wasn't much of a clue anyway. A girlfriend and a Limestone Canyon flyer—big deal. The whole thing was beginning to seem faraway after two days, but then I got a call from Melissa Montalli. Melissa is always stirring things up, although she did so inadvertently in this case. She works part-time for the county planning commission and consults on the side, so she has a finger in every environmental pie in the region, including the Limestone Canyon Defense Council. Melissa had a job for me. How would I like to supply trees for a stream rehabilitation project she was putting together? I'd love to if I could get paid. Of course, I'd get paid: it was a government grant. In that case I'd want 50 percent up front and 18 percent interest on deferred payments. Merry laughter.

"Melissa, have you been to any meetings of the Limestone Canyon Defense Council recently?"

"I really haven't had time."

"Any in the past year?"

"I think I went to one in January."

"Was somebody there named Blackwell, by any chance?"

"Blackwell?"

"A biologist. From the Bayview Museum."

"Not that I recall. Why?"

"I'd like to know if he was involved with Limestone Canyon."

"Grenville has Fred Bell behind him now, you know. He's talking about hydroelectric again." Fred Bell was a state legislator who spent a lot of time talking about solar energy and salmon rehabilitation, and a lot of time listening to timber industry lobbyists. "Is this Blackwell a friend of yours?"

"He was. He's dead now."

"Oh. You should talk to Ed Sorenson. He's the chairman now." She gave me Sorenson's number and said she had a lot of other calls to make. People don't like to ask about the dead. Might be unlucky.

Ed Sorenson proved hard to contact, which was provocative.

The harder people are to reach, the more they have to tell, as a general rule. After the ninth phone call—five busy signals, three unanswered, and one faulty connection—I was ready for something good.

"You mean the guy from the Bayview Museum?" Sorenson had a calm, slightly reedy voice, redolent of small-town business. He was a pharmacist in Weaverville. "I was wondering what happened to him. He was going to send me a report on some field work he was doing in the canyon."

"Unfortunately he's been killed." I couldn't bring myself to say "murdered."

"Killed? In the canyon?"

"No. In Oakland."

"I'm sorry to hear that. He seemed like a nice fellow."

"Did he say what fieldwork he was doing?"

"Well, no. It wasn't just Limestone Canyon. He said he was doing the whole north side of the Trinitys. He said something—there were anomalies—but I don't know much about this. Why do you ask?"

"I'm a friend of his." A pause. "Have you been to Limestone Canyon recently, Mr. Sorenson?"

"No, I'm ashamed to say I haven't. Used to go all the time when I was younger. We had a cabin over west of Cecilville. It's such a long drive; I haven't had time."

"Well, thanks, Mr. Sorenson."

"You know, you should talk to Fred Cooley, the biologist with the Forest Service. He'd probably be able to tell you more about what your friend was up to."

I did indeed know that I should talk to Fred Cooley, but I didn't particularly want to. People who work for the Forest Service around here get a kind of special tone in their voices when they talk to me, as though I might drop my pants at any moment. It's a severe tone with some, an amused tone with others. Fred was one of the amused ones. He's one of those intelligent, reasonable people who somehow fit into stupid, senseless institutions. I got Fred on the first phone call.

"Limestone Canyon? Yeah, I was up there a couple years ago. Good steelhead stream. Too bad."

"There's nothing unusual about it?"

"Not that I know of. Which doesn't mean there isn't. It hasn't been surveyed very extensively, unless your friend did some exploring. He never talked to me anyway."

"Never spoke to you at all?"

"Nope. You say he was killed in Oakland?"

"Yeah."

"Well, I wouldn't go into Limestone Canyon right now."

"Yeah?"

"Lots of bad feeling around there. You know. Outside agitators. Carpetbaggers."

Limestone Canyon was getting increasingly interesting. There's nothing like being warned away from a place to make you want to go see it. I got out my map of Trinity National Forest, which fell apart as I unfolded it. I fitted back the fallen pieces and sat down to contemplate the Salmon Trinity Alps, the second biggest roadless area in California. After all these years, I still get a thrill every time I see its vaguely winged shape on a map, even a tacky, unreliable Forest Service one.

After some enjoyable mental sauntering over the likes of Megram Ridge, Petrified Gulch, and Hangers Roost Camp, I located Limestone Canyon: near Cecilville, as Sorenson had said, with Plummer and St. Claire creeks to the east and west of it and Limestone Bluffs and Limestone Ridge to the north and south of it. The creek that had eroded the canyon, appropriately if unimaginatively called Limestone Creek, headed at the Salmon Trinity Crest and ran northward into the main fork of the Salmon River.

I saw right away one reason why the canyon's defenders were having a hard time. It was in an administrative limbo, partly in one national forest, partly in another. The Salmon Trinity Crest makes a nice, simple boundary between Klamath and Trinity national forests, except at Limestone Canyon. Limestone Creek heads much farther south than the other streams on the Salmon drainage, pointing a finger down into the Trinity drainage.

It must have been a problem for the administrators who laid out the forests. Should they put a kink in their nice, straight east-west boundary to keep the Limestone Creek headwaters in Klamath National Forest along with the rest of the Salmon drainage? They decided against kinks. They put the upper third of Limestone Canyon in Trinity National Forest and the lower two-thirds in Klamath National Forest. The white squares of Pierre Grenville's inholdings in the lower part of the canyon are under a different supervisor than the upper part of the canyon. Grenville didn't have to divide to conquer; it had been done for him.

It was a long drive over there, as Sorenson had said. Most of a day: I'd have to drive all the way around the roadless area. Of course, it would be about a fourth as long a distance if I went across the roadless area, but that would take four days of walking, even if there was a trail across the Salmon Trinity divide into Limestone Creek, which there wasn't. There didn't seem to be any trails into Limestone Canyon at all.

I went back to planting seeds, but Limestone Canyon kept nagging. Nothing was going on otherwise. Alec Rice seemed to have been a flash in the pan. Lots of people can get excited about having their land reforested without ever actually *doing* anything about it. Sometimes I think they drag me up to their property just so I'll admire it. Anything for an audience.

Even Grunewald seemed to have forgotten me, for which I felt duly grateful, though perhaps just the faintest bit let down. Anything for an audience, even a disapproving one. I decided I really needed some exercise. Maybe I could do some fishing. It would be a good pretext if somebody proved disagreeable.

Chapter Nine

THE NEXT MORNING I gave Lewis a big breakfast, put a lot of cat food on the porch, said a prayer to the god of automatic sprinkler timers, and set out for Limestone Canyon. I stopped for coffee in Weaverville at the cafe where Diane had worked.

"Well hello, George," said Wanda, the owner, "where've you been hiding?"

"Under a rock."

"You do look kind of pasty."

"Thanks, Wanda." Wanda doesn't like me for what I did to Diane. Divorcing her, that is. If she knew what I really did, she'd like me less. "I'm on my way to get a tan."

"Going fishing? Got a license?"

"Of course."

"Let's see."

"What? You the new warden?"

"Somebody's got to keep an eye on you."

As I was driving out of town, I passed Rodrigo in the two-seater pickup. He didn't appear to see me, just looked ahead with a kind of stolid intensity. He certainly was a large man. I wondered where he was going. He was headed in the direction of my place. I wondered if I was being summoned again and thought of turning back. The idea of Rodrigo poking around my place didn't appeal to me. I kept on going, though. I hate turning back once I've set a course, which makes me resolute or inflexible, depending on the point of view.

I drove north past the dead, red banks of Clair Engle Lake to Callahan in lonesome Scott Valley, then west to Cecilville, the country getting greener, bushier, and steeper the farther west I went. It was like driving around an enormous, jagged rock wall, "alp piled on alp," as the dismayed beaver trappers of the Hudson's Bay Company complained when they first saw the Trinitys. The road was gravel for the last few miles west of Cecilville, which is an old mining town, nothing much now but a Forest Service station and a general store for summer people.

It was late when I finally located the canyon's mouth, so I pulled down to the riverbank, lit up the hibachi I'd brought, and treated myself to a steak and some nice zinfandel. The setting wasn't quite as sylvan as I'd expected. Somebody with hard-bitten tastes in landscaping lived across the road. A taut-strung barbed wire fence enclosed a property eaten bare by livestock and littered with the usual rural junk. In the middle sat a large, new aluminum-sided house unencumbered with flowerbeds or shade trees. An enormous air-conditioning unit on the roof looked as though it ate kilowatts for breakfast. No wonder they wanted a hydroelectric dam on Limestone Creek. I'd have expected a pack of curs to bad-mouth me from that setting, but it seemed deserted.

Dusk gathers fast in these canyons, even in late spring. After watching the first shift of bats chase each other over the river, I crawled into the back of the truck and dozed off. Later I was awakened by a great rumbling and flashing in the dust as a huge pickup with balloon tires, searchlights, and all kinds of other gizmos pulled into the property across the road. But that disturbance subsided, and I got back to sleep after watching the stars for a while.

I woke with the anticipation I always feel for a day in the woods, once all the hassles of getting to the woods are over. That I had a mission, albeit a vague one, made it even better because it quieted the mental buzzings of guilt-at-idleness that have pursued me, like humming-bird-size harpies, all the way from old New England. It was a perfect morning. The birds were still singing as I started up what seemed like a pretty good trail into the canyon. There hadn't been a trail on my Forest Service map, but that didn't surprise me.

These canyons are full of western tanagers, black-headed grosbeaks, and solitary vireos: colorful birds that look very different but all sound vaguely like robins. If bird song serves to repel rivals of the same species from nesting territories, you'd think they'd have different songs. But maybe they just sound like robins to ignorant human ears. It's mysterious. The canyons are good places for mysteries, with all their leafy twistings and turnings. The virgin ones tend to be so overhung with big Douglas firs and canyon live oaks as to be permanently in shadow, but they don't seem gloomy because of all the bright green maples, ashes, and alders that grow beside the creeks. Looking down into one, you get an impression of brightness underlying dimness, as though the light comes from the gravel and boulders of the creekbed instead of the sky.

I walked along, having a good time thinking thoughts and listening to birds. There were hermit thrushes singing too, way back in the side canyons. Then the trail started to disintegrate. Poetic thoughts are not possible on a disintegrating trail. First there were landslides, which I crossed in undignified haste at the risk of falling into the creekbed a hundred or so feet below. Then canyon live oaks had overgrown the trail. I had to crawl under them, and there's nothing stiffer or pricklier to crawl under. Luckily I was carrying a rucksack instead of a backpack. Then I came to where a very large (what my piss-fir friends would call "overmature") Douglas fir had fallen across. When I'd climbed over that, I had to elbow my way through a horde of its offspring that had overgrown the other side as though huddled together to mourn their fallen parent.

Then the trail forked, and forked again, and again, fraying into a web of deer paths that led exuberantly nowhere: to cliff edges or impenetrable brush or slopes too steep for a biped. Deer must be carefree creatures, judging from their trails. They seem under no compulsion to *get* much of anywhere. Bear trails are much more purposeful, in keeping with the moroseness of bears.

Bears apparently had enough sense to stay out of Limestone Canyon. I finally gave up on the trail and dropped into the creekbed, and when I say dropped, I mean *dropped*. I plummeted from one overhanging tree to another like a vertical Tarzan and scared hell out of the local water ouzel when I abruptly came to rest on a sandbar. The ouzel flew away, and I sat down for a rest. It was getting late in the morning and pretty warm, even in the shady canyon. I didn't know how far upstream I'd come, but I was afraid it wasn't far. Bad trails take up a lot of time. Creek bottoms take even more, with boulders, waterfalls, timber jams, and potholes. I didn't want to spend more than a day at this. I started walking, wading, and crawling upstream.

A few places were as bad as I'd expected, but I was pleasantly surprised. Cutting through soft limestone, the creek was less choked with big rocks than creeks that run through granite or schist. There were boulders, the steep slopes above guaranteed that, but much of the bed was gentle and U-shaped, with low, stair-step waterfalls and bone-colored rock walls full of the calcareous sea creatures that had died to make them in the Mesozoic era. The walls sometimes closed in on deep pools under the waterfalls, which I had to climb around or swim across, not easy with a pack, even a light one.

The pools were chilly but interesting. They reminded me a little of the limestone sinks they have in Florida. Rocky shelves overhung indigo cavities from which the loglike tails of summer steelheads occasionally protruded, and circular aquamarine holes seemed to open (or perhaps it was just a trick of shadows) into deeper pools where no bottom was visible. The colors were unusual for the Trinitys, where pools usually look dark green. These looked blue, perhaps because the limestone reflected light differently than the more common igneous and metamorphic rocks.

I could see why Grenville wanted to dam the creek. Its relatively gentle gradient would make it easy. I could see why people who'd been there wanted him not to. But I couldn't see anything that would make headlines. You don't usually grab the media by saying that a place has sort of interesting and unusual geology, with nice deep pools a slightly different color than the next creek over. If it had hot springs, that might be something. But the water was normally icy for a Salmon drainage creek. Being on the north side of the Trinitys, the Salmon drainage gets a lot of snowmelt.

What might Blackwell have been looking for? Something herpetological, which could be all kinds of things: snakes, turtles, lizards, frogs, toads, salamanders—weird things like caecilians and amphiumas. He specialized in salamanders. Were caecilians and amphiumas salamanders too? I thought maybe amphiumas were. Where would this thing he was looking for live (assuming he *was* looking)? Under logs? Underground? Underwater?

I had some lunch, feeling lame brained. How many logs can you turn over in an afternoon? There had to be *something* to go on. I thought of Grunewald's charred scraps of paper. Something blue with some kind of grooves. Grooves characteristic of salamanders. So, blue salamanders, which might, of course, live under logs, underground, or underwater. Or fifty feet up in trees. Was it something Blackwell had *found* or just something he was looking for? But if he hadn't found it, how did he know it was blue? If he did know it was blue.

The creek babbled, the cicadas buzzed in the trees: my mind made similar sounds. Then I decided, the hell with it; I'd do what I felt like doing. What did I feel like doing? Not like scrambling around on the slopes turning over logs. If Blackwell wanted blue rattlesnakes, he could have them. I might just give up and do some fishing. I'd brought the gear. But what if there *was* something here?

It was warmer than ever, and the pools were beginning to look inviting, cold as they were. I'd seen salamanders in them, nothing unusual, just the common Pacific giant salamanders and

66

rough-skinned newts, neither of which have any blue on them. If Blackwell's find was in the water, I'd at least stand a chance of seeing it, which I wouldn't if it was underground. I took off my clothes, put on a pair of sneakers, left rucksack and hiking boots in a sheltered spot, and started upstream, hopefully carrying a plastic container I'd brought.

It was discouraging. I didn't see anything unusual in the shallow pools, and I couldn't see anything at all in the deep ones, not from the surface. The logical thing to do, then, was to dive into the deep pools. I'd always thought diving for treasure or rare animals sounded agreeable, and it probably would have been if I'd had a wet suit, snorkel, and goggles. Without them it was not much fun. The water was cold enough at the surface; it was like the hand of death a dozen feet down. I couldn't see anything to speak of at that depth. I groped around in the ooze or gravel until I ran out of air or got panicky at the chill and gloom. Then I'd lie gasping on a sandbar until I began to feel warm-blooded again.

I get into a feedback cycle in situations like this. When I can't stand it anymore, I tell myself I'll try once more because the one last time seems lucky. I still don't come up with anything, but I tell myself I'll try just one *last* time, and so on. It keeps me going, up to a point.

I thought I'd just about reached that point when I came to a particularly deep pool under a particularly high waterfall. Then I though that if I didn't explore this one, it would bother me; whereas if I did explore it and then turned right around and went home without seeing the next pool upstream, I'd feel better. I dived dutifully in and didn't even make it to the bottom on the first try. It was like diving into a Tom Collins with all the effervescence from the water, a Tom Collins with lots of ice. I crawled out and gasped for a while. The sun was getting low, what I could see of it through the trees. I decided that if I just *touched* the bottom, I could quit. I jumped up and down a few times, cursed the universe, dived in, and touched bottom. I wasn't feeling completely numb and smothered yet, and it really *was* my last dive, so I groped around a little, and touched some-thing soft that moved.

It moved, of course, out of reach. I grabbed mud, scratched my thumb on a submerged branch, and returned to the surface. More sprawling and gasping. It probably was a newt or a giant salamander. I hadn't given much thought to how I'd *catch* some-thing once I'd found it. I went into my feedback cycle again and handled lots of mud and submerged branches.

Then, as I was rising to the surface for the *absolute last* time, just where the watery shadows gave way to watery sunlight, something swam past my head, so close that it almost touched me. Something blue? My hands went out in a kind of despairing reflex and closed around something soft that moved. It didn't move out of reach *this* time. It's a good thing that salamanders have pliable, cartilaginous skeletons. I held on very tight.

I kicked my way to the shallows, stood up, and lifted from the water a creature that seemed made of turquoise and lapis lazuli, with ruby belly and topaz eyes. It was shaped more or less like a salamander, but it wasn't any species I'd seen. If it hadn't been moving, I'd have thought it was some kind of gem-encrusted statue. The colors were that fresh and pure. Fish and amphibi-ans often have a kind of resplendence just after they've been taken from the water, but this was more than that, this was *resplendence*.

Such colors fade quickly in death, even in captivity. I felt a strong impulse to release the creature, but I suppressed it. I'd paid for this. I scooped water into my container, dumped the creature in, and hurried back downstream, stopping periodically to put fresh water in the container. The creature took this as amphibians take most things—phlegmatically.

It was getting dark when I reached the truck. The creature still seemed all right: still blue. I drove back through the night, sleeping by the road for a few hours, and arrived in Weaverville in time to get breakfast at Wanda's (who looked knowing when I said I hadn't caught any fish) and an aquarium setup at the local pet store.

I had my captive installed in the barn by the afternoon, after some feverish work to rig up a fresh-water circulation system for the aquarium. I was glad my water comes from a spring instead of a chlorinated municipal system. As I worked, Lewis demanded entrance, sniffed at my exertions, peered too interestedly into the aquarium, and was expelled with a rudeness that he took philosophically, as cats take most things.

Chapter Ten

I GOT OUT my copy of Stebbins's *Field Guide to Western Reptiles and Amphibians*. There were some pretty salamanders in it, but there weren't any turquoise and lapis lazuli ones. One subspecies of the long-toed salamander, *Ambystoma gracilis*, was greenish, if not blue; but that subspecies wasn't supposed to live in the Trinitys and doesn't get more than three inches long, not counting the tail. My blue creature was at least five. The more I compared it with the salamanders in Stebbins's book, the odder it looked. It wasn't just the color: it wasn't shaped quite like the others.

I thought of phoning Dr. Todd at the museum, but I was hungry and tired. I hastily cooked and ate an omelette, which made me feel sleepy. I could call Todd later. I turned the air-conditioner down low, lay down in bed for a little nap, and slept for twelve hours.

I was awakened by the telephone. It was Alec Rice. He sounded impatient.

"Where've you been?" he said. "I thought you were going to bring me a reforestation plan."

"Uhh?"

"Sorry if I got you out of bed."

"That's all right. Yeah, uh, sure. I will."

"Why don't you bring it up today? Let me see it."

"Uh, I haven't done it yet."

"Haven't done it?"

"I need to make a survey of your land. Get maps."

"Of course. I wasn't thinking. Well, come up today and get started. I've got maps. You can make me an estimate, and I'll advance you some cash."

It was abrupt, maybe even a little peremptory, but I wasn't about to refuse an offer of cash. First I went out to the barn to check on the creature. It seemed all right: still blue, still moving. I wasn't sure what it ate. I'd bought some live brine shrimp at the aquarium store. I put some in. The creature didn't react with enthusiasm; in fact, it didn't react at all, but cold-blooded animals aren't noted for voracious appetites. Their metabolisms are too slow to require much fuel: lucky for us warm-blooded animals. Imagine a world of *really* hungry snakes and crocodiles. Anyway, the creature was alive and not conspicuously unhealthy. I rushed off to make money.

Alec was in a genial mood when I arrived. I sensed that he was one of those people who turn charm on and off at will. It's not necessarily a bad trait: most successful people have it to some degree. Still, it made me wonder again why he was being so accommodating to me. He had all the maps and acreages and other information right there. I also wondered why he put Jimmy and Rodrigo at my disposal for the whole day. They evidently weren't thrilled with the assignment.

It was a full day's job just to get a look at the ranch, much less to figure out exposures, slopes, elevations, and soil types. It was a good place for growing trees, no doubt about it: lots of fairly level ridgelines; wide benches over the creeks; deep, moist soils; and an extensive and stable road system. And no cattle, if Alec was sincere.

"Man, I don't believe this place," said Jimmy as we trudged along one more brushy ridgeline. Rodrigo had stayed in the truck, obviously bored.

"What do you mean?"

"It's so empty. I thought the U.S. was supposed to be one big

71

city, skyscrapers and cars everywhere, people riding around in helicopters."

"It's a big country."

"Too big, man. Too empty. There aren't even any animals here. You don't see nothing but a few deer and squirrels, and little gray birds that go 'peek-peek.' If this was Guatemala, in a wild place like this, you'd see all kinds of different birds, monkeys, iguanas. All kinds of stuff."

"Seen any bears?"

"Hey, I don't know if I want to see one of those. They come around at night. We see their tracks. Big tracks."

"They're pretty harmless. How about mountain lions?"

"You mean puma? I saw one in Guatemala once. In *la selva*, the Petén. Really beautiful."

"It's pretty country, though, isn't it?"

"Oh yeah. It looks like parts of Guatemala, in the mountains. But too cold, man, too empty. Didn't Indians ever live here?"

"Oh yeah. But white settlers killed most of them a long time ago. Then the settlers couldn't make a living here, so they sold the land to a few rich people."

"Sounds like Guatemala, except they're still killing the Indians there."

We heard Rodrigo calling something in Spanish. Jimmy answered him impatiently. I wondered about the relationship between them. It wasn't very genial, although they seemed to spend most of their time together. Rodrigo was stiff and silent, and Jimmy kept saying mocking things about him in English, about what a big, dumb macho he was.

"What does he want?"

"He wants to know where we are. He's afraid maybe a bear will eat us. He has to protect us."

"That's why he's got that armory in the truck?"

"He loves guns, man, guns and knives. You know what his ambition is?"

"What?"

72

"To kill a shark with a knife. They do that in the Philippines to prove their manhood."

"I'm surprised he hasn't done it already."

"Hey, sharks are smart, man. They stay away from him."

"I thought deer seemed kind of scarce around here."

"Oh yeah. He shoots anything he sees."

"Doesn't Alec mind?"

"Alec likes to shoot."

"You don't?"

"They're good for some things, guns. I'd rather just walk in the woods, though. Too noisy. Too much hassle."

"I thought you didn't like these woods."

"In the summer they're not so bad. Peaceful."

I thought of asking Jimmy again why he worked for Alec, but I supposed he'd have told me the first time if he wanted me to know. If Alec wanted to decimate his deer, it was his business. It would make my job easier. I've had too many painfully nur-tured seedlings nipped in the bud to be too solicitous about deer.

The sun was setting as we drove back to the ranch headquar-ters. Jimmy turned to look at the western horizon, which had some clouds in it, unusual for the time of year. They weren't very impressive: gunpowder gray and dull violet against the faded orange of the sky.

"Your sunsets up here sure are long and boring," he said. "If this was Guatemala, that sky would be like a wild turkey's tail. We got these wild turkeys in the Petén with tails that are all different colors, purple and blue and yellow. One minute the sky is plain blue, the next it's like a wild turkey's tail, the next it's black. None of this hanging around. You want to see a sunset, you go out about six, you damned well see a sunset."

Alec invited me in for a drink when we got back. Wendy was there, dressed in jeans, cowboy boots, and a western shirt. She seemed in a better mood than last time. We made some chitchat about how big and pretty the ranch was. The house was a lot more comfortable than it looked from the outside. Alec, or some-

73

body, had stripped away the moldy wallboard and linoleum, insulated and plastered the walls, put down hardwood floors, and filled the rooms with expensive furniture, rugs, and appliances. The drinks were comfortable too: high-class liquor, the kind you see advertised in the *New Yorker*.

"So," said Alec, "what's it going to cost me to reforest this place?"

"Depends how much you want to reforest."

"I told you, I want to reforest all of it."

"Well, I'd be lying to you if I told you it was all fit to be reforested. A lot of it is, most of it, but there're parts that will never grow commercial timber."

"How much will the parts that *will* cost?"

"I haven't figured that out yet."

"Why didn't you say so?" He got up and went into the next room for a moment, then came back and sat down. "How's the tree business, anyway?"

"Not bad."

"Not good?"

"It's not a blue-chip stock."

"How's your capital?"

"Why do you ask?"

"I don't like to see worthy enterprises going under. So many of them do. Have another?"

"All right."

Alec went to his bar and mixed me a whiskey and soda with his usual absorption. After handing it to me, he looked me in the eye again as he'd done on the knoll during my first visit. This time, with some whiskey under my belt, I looked resolutely back. I was glad Wendy had left the room after the conversation had turned to business. I felt ridiculous, but Alec obviously didn't. He returned to his chair and picked up the conversation where he'd left it.

"Ever think about diversifying?"

"Uh, yeah. You could say I'd thought about it."

"One-crop economies are so vulnerable."

"Boll weevils."

"Precisely. There's a statue to the boll weevil in some Texas town. Taught them to diversify. I heard about some farmers down in the valley that are interplanting Indian hemp with corn, getting two crops from one piece of ground. Food and fiber."

"You planning to grow corn up here?" Alec shrugged, a little impatiently. Wendy had gone into the kitchen, from which very pleasant smells emanated.

"Why don't you stay for dinner?" Alec said. "In fact, stay the night. You can dream how many trees you want to plant, and I'll give you a down payment in the morning."

"I've got some things to take care of at home."

"You're not the kind of person who's afraid to dream, are you? Opportunity knocks once."

"I'll stay if you'll stop spouting platitudes."

"Ha ha ha." Alec's laugh was not his greatest charm. He went to the outside door and shouted in Spanish. Pretty soon Jimmy and Rodrigo came in and started setting the table. The dinner, which arrived efficiently, was extraordinary. Wendy must have been professionally trained. Quail on toast, then roast saddle of venison. Three wines. Nobody said where the quail and venison came from, but I doubted they'd been sent up from San Francisco, although I didn't bite on any shotgun pellets.

"My god, do you eat like this all the time?"

"You mean do we always eat game out of season?"

"No, I mean do you always eat so well."

"Life's too short to eat badly. That's another platitude isn't it? We all have to watch what we say now so as not to offend George's ear for platitudes." Everybody went on eating, but I felt the stiffening that comes over a group as a tyrant starts to assert himself. Even Rodrigo seemed to sense it. Wendy made some innocent, changing-the-subject remark and brought trouble on herself.

"Poor Wendy won't be able to say anything. Say something that's not a platitude, Wendy." Wendy kept her eyes on her plate. Jimmy glanced at me. Alec leaned back in his chair. "Let

75

me see, what can I say that's not a platitude?" He looked at the ceiling. "Here's something. Economics precludes ecology. That's a truism but not a platitude. Don't you agree?"

"More or less."

"So why are you in the tree business? You've been precluded."

"Just frivolous, I guess."

"You are frivolous, George. You should take heed. Here's a history lesson for you, starting with an epigram, though you may think it's merely a simile. Cultures are like isotopes; they disintegrate at varying rates. I've been a student of Latin American culture for many years, as Jimmy and Rodrigo can tell you, and I've seen that culture's rate of disintegration get out of hand. It's just going too fast down there. It used to be very comfortable, very favorable for untaxed agricultural development. Just the right institutional corruption, just the right fiscal chaos, just the right rural poverty. But it's changing too fast now. People aren't going to believe how fast it's been changing.

"On the other hand, look what we've got up here. It's beginning to ripen up here. An underfunded, increasingly impotent and potentially very corrupt bureaucracy. An alienated, increasingly impoverished rural population. A used-up resource base dominated by absentee ownership. Plenty of cutover back country with dirt roads, courtesy of the timber industry. No guerrillas. It's nice to be home. Things are going to be good here for a long time. I like the idea of a little stability and permanence now."

"Some other people have these ideas."

"But I've got capital. It just grows: it's like a chain reaction. That's why you got out, isn't it? You were afraid of being run over by capital. I value somebody with the brains to see that. But you don't have to be run over if you have some support. You've seen what I've got here. You could run it for me. We don't need the tropics for all-year operations with solar and geothermal options. I'm looking at other parcels too."

Wendy and Jimmy looked a little surprised at the direction

76

the conversation was taking. I gathered that my host didn't offer a kind of junior partnership to every guest he had at his dinner table. Alec was looking flushed. He certainly had moved quickly from a sullen mood to an expansive one, but the food and wine would do that. I was feeling a little expansive myself. It's nice to see your potential recognized, even by an apparently somewhat-unbalanced criminal. Who's balanced these days, anyway? Alec's ideas weren't impossible: imaginative maybe, but not impossible. I stayed cool, though.

"Sounds awfully complicated," I said.

"Yeah, but the markets. The *markets.* You have to industrialize. They aren't saturated, you know. A little soft here, but think about this: There's Japan. Japan is *us* in 1960. And once you're in Japan, you're in Asia. Korea, Manchuria, Siberia. The Soviet Union, man. China. Things aren't going to get any easier for the Asians. They're going to need help once they get bored with cameras and bullet trains."

"What about the law?"

"Decreasingly a factor here. It's getting too expensive, and it'll be a long time before things get bad enough for real destabilization. I had no problems with the law down there. It's those god-damned *descamisados* with their AK-47s that get on my nerves. Not that they won't do business at times, but they're unpredictable. Like all barbarians. You know what Mao did to the opium industry."

"Latin Americans aren't barbarians."

"No more than the people who sacked Rome were barbarians. They were smelting metal in northern Europe when the Romans were still living on acorns. They're from a different culture, so they're barbarians. They think *we're* barbarians. Right, Jimmy? Hell, they still practice courtesy and charity down there, when they aren't chopping heads. Ask Jimmy. Nicest guy in the world until the fit comes on him, then watch out for that machete. Hey, compadre?"

"Sure thing, jefe."

"Don't let Jimmy fool you with his *ladino* act. Jimmy has an education. Jimmy's going to get rich, just like me. Don't you want to get rich, George? House in Switzerland? Villa in Spain?"

"I'm certainly willing to give it some very serious consideration."

"Ha ha ha. Yes, you should consider it. I can't spend that much time here. You like the country life: you could manage it. Grow things the way you like, with substantial commissions and salary too. No overhead, job security, lots of benefits. I think you retired too early."

"What about Jimmy and Rodrigo?"

"Jimmy and Rodrigo don't have their green cards yet. Their status is a little indeterminate." Jimmy said something rapidly in Spanish, and Rodrigo looked at Alec questioningly. Alec didn't respond. He stood up a little heavily. He'd drunk a good deal, but then so had I. "Wendy will show you to the guest room. I've got some calls to make."

Wendy led me down the passage to a room that hadn't been renovated yet. It had pink floral linoleum and pink wallboard. I could imagine some ranch wife thinking it was real pretty back in 1933.

"Is he always like that at the dinner table?"

"What do you mean?" Wendy folded her arms.

"Well, uh. Autocratic."

"His shoulder is bothering him."

"His shoulder?"

"An old injury. Goodnight." Wendy gave me a big airline stewardess smile and disappeared. She wasn't going to chat about Alec with me, which probably meant she was afraid of him, though it could mean other things.

It wasn't that late, but the nightlife was over, evidently. I heard something walking lightly across the gravel outside and looked through the window, but I couldn't see anything. I wondered if it was one of the dogs that Alec kept in a pen beside the barn. They were Dobermans, hard to see at night. I decided against a moonlight stroll. I was tired anyway.

78

I took off my shoes and lay on the bed, which seemed to have been in the room as long as the linoleum. I guessed that Alec didn't get too many guests. I didn't know what to make of his "job offer." It might have been a goodwill gesture, or a joke, or a putdown. Casual offers of that sort put the maker of the offer at an advantage because they place all the responsibility for following through on the recipient. I wondered if I could get Wendy thrown in with the deal. It seemed unlikely that she would want to stay in the place any more than Alec did. I really didn't think I did either, not with Dobermans prowling under my windows at night.

I cheered up when I thought of Alec's promised check, a more substantial offer, I hoped. I took out my notebook and my handy pocket calculator and started running up the figures. The light in the room wasn't the best, though—one naked overhead bulb—and my eyelids got heavy after a while. I turned it off and slept, dreaming of little green numbers appearing and disappearing in a black rectangle, numbers that mounted up to some very heartening sums.

I awoke in the dark. At first all I could hear was my heart pounding and the air rasping in my nostrils, then I heard other things. Barking and snarling, the Dobermans; but there were other sounds, high-pitched yammering and squealing. Pigs? Something ran past the window, then ran back again, pursued by something that seemed to be giggling in an owlish sort of way. A loud burst of growling, snarling, and howling erupted over the entire compound, it seemed. Then gunfire, *automatic* gunfire, for God's sake. I saw the crackling flashes of it silhouetting trees and outbuildings, then I hit the floor. There were a few more gunfire bursts, some shouting in Spanish, diminishing howls, then silence.

I got up and looked out the window. It was quite dark and still, as though nothing had happened. There was no sound from the house, even when I went to my door and listened. No concerned or questioning murmurs, just dead silence. Apparently Alec was unconcerned. For some reason that was more unnerving than screams in the night. I decided I'd stay in a tent when tree-planting time came around. I began to wonder about holding onto tree-planting crews.

I concealed my anxieties the next morning, except for asking Alec what the noise had been about.

"It's the goddamned coyotes," he said. "They keep trying to fuck the dogs."

"Brave coyotes."

"Fuck them or eat them, we're not sure which. Maybe a little of both. Sometimes we come out in the morning and one of the dogs is covered with saliva, just dripping with it. Like they'd tried to swallow her whole."

"Did they shoot any last night?"

"You kidding? They dodge the bullets."

"Maybe you should keep the dogs penned at night."

Alec didn't answer. Wendy made omelettes, and we all ate heartily. I decided not to mention Alec's managerial offer, and he didn't bring it up. He talked at length to Wendy about a phone conversation he'd had the night before, something about some computer software investments, all very legal and dull.

I was getting ready to mention my estimate, but Alec asked me first. No reluctance there. He listened to my pitch, whipped out his checkbook, and wrote me a check for a third of it, the biggest check I'd seen in the tree business, or any business since I'd sold the house. I hung around for a while after that, suppressing a desire to kiss his feet, but he'd finished with me for the present, so I ran along.

Chapter Eleven

I WENT TO the barn to check on the creature when I got home. It was gone: no creature, no aquarium, no filtration system, except for the line I'd run to the nearest faucet. If that hadn't still been there, dangling like a severed air hose (the thief had been considerate enough to turn off the faucet), the whole thing would have been like a dream. Lewis followed me into the barn, looking surprised, but then he always looks a little surprised. *I* was surprised. I hadn't even thought to lock the barn.

Nothing else was missing; nothing was broken or damaged. It evidently wasn't a random theft. In fact, it was openly purposeful, in a way a message from somebody. It made me think, which I hadn't been doing too much as I rushed about collecting salamanders and reforestation checks. It's pretty rare to be touched by an openly purposeful act, particularly such an aggressive and threatening one. Society may be a web of aggression, of property as theft, but it's dusty with legalistic normality, so we forget there are spiders in it.

Blackwell had discovered an unknown, or at least a very rare creature in Limestone Creek, apparently hadn't told anybody, and had been murdered. Would somebody kill for a salamander, even if it was unknown or rare and did live in a creek that some people wanted badly to dam? It seemed unlikely, or at least unconventional. Of course, I had a way of finding out. I also had found the unknown or rare creature in Limestone Creek. I also had told nobody. I phoned Grunewald. He wasn't there, of course. I phoned Dr. Todd at the Bayview, as I wished I had two days before, when I had something to show him. He was interested in the creature, politely noncommittal about its disappearance.

"A *blue* salamander?"

"Really blue, like semiprecious stone."

"There's the blue-spotted salamander back east. Somebody might have transplanted some."

"Eight or nine inches long with the tail."

"A bit large. Dark bluish black with paler blue specks, like an old enameled coffeepot?"

"More turquoise with dark blue blotches."

"Doesn't sound like the blue-spotted. Well, there's no reason it shouldn't be a new species. If any new vertebrate species shows up, it's likely to be a salamander. Secretive habits." The prospect exhilarated him mildly. Dr. Todd was an entomologist. He passed the buck: not much else he could do. "You know, there's a woman living up there somewhere who's an authority. She discovered a new salamander a few years ago. In Costa Rica. Or maybe it was Bolivia. She was down here a couple of years ago helping us with our collections. Very bright gal. I think I have her address here somewhere. Shriver? Shrove?"

"Carla Shreve?"

"That's it. Do you know her?"

"No."

"You probably should talk to her." A pause. "Now where—." Shuffling of papers. "Just a minute." A longer pause. Todd sounded exasperated when he came back on. "I'll have to get back to you. My directory seems to have gotten snowed under."

"I'd appreciate it." I was just a little disappointed at his sangfroid, but I suppose people call up museums about "new" species they've discovered fairly often. I'd had the fantasy myself a few times: ranger discovers nocturnal ape-man, forester flaunts fabled find.

Grunewald returned my call and listened to my tale of woe in silence. It's disconcerting to tell a story to a listener who doesn't help you along with little grunts and interjections and expressions of polite interest. I suppose that's why he did it. My confidence wasn't enhanced by the necessity of talking around my purloining of the Save Limestone Canyon flyer. Grunewald went right for that little weak point.

"How did you find out about this canyon?"

"Somebody up here told me about it."

"Who?"

"A woman named Melissa Montalli."

"Spell it." I did. "What was her connection to Blackwell?"

"I don't know. She met him at a meeting."

"You didn't by any chance find something while you were poking around in your friend's office?"

"Somebody had cleaned it out."

"So I heard."

"Did you ever find out who?" The best defense . . .

"I'm the one who's investigating this crime, Kilgore."

"Just trying to be helpful."

"Did you tell your sheriff's office about this theft?" I hadn't. "You expect me to drive up there and look into it for you?"

"There's no need to be sarcastic."

"You'd better get your sheriff's department over there. There's nothing we can do for you. Your friend's on the back burner down here. We've got three new ones already, one in the back of the head."

"You think they're related?"

"Hah. Call your sheriff." I said I would, but I didn't. Somehow I just couldn't see the local deputies investigating a theft complaint about a pretty blue salamander, especially a complaint from the likes of me.

"What kind of salamander was it, Mr. Kilgore, sir?"

"Well, you see it was a kind of salamander that hasn't been discovered yet, so it doesn't have a name. So I don't actually know what kind of salamander it was, assuming it is a salamander, which I don't know either. It *looked* like a salamander."

"What else might it have been, Mr. Kilgore?"

"Gee, I don't know."

"Could it have been a dinosaur or a basilisk?"

"Well, gosh."

I had another course of action open to me, but I wasn't eager to take it. I could go back to Limestone Canyon for another creature. But whoever had known I had a Limestone Canyon salamander the first time would be quite likely to know if I had one a second time. If they'd steal, they might do other things. They might do them in Limestone Canyon.

I tried burying myself in Alec's juicy timber plan, but I couldn't keep my attention focused. A funny coincidence, my having spent the night at Alec's as the creature was being stolen. Of course, it meant that Alec hadn't stolen it, unless he'd put on a pretty elaborate show that night. What could Alec have to do with damming Limestone Canyon? Hydroelectric options? It seemed a little remote.

I had a nagging sense that what I did about the creature might really matter somehow. It was disagreeable. I told myself that somebody else would discover the creatures, that they probably wouldn't dam Limestone Creek for a long time, if ever, and that the creatures must also live somewhere else anyway. But it all sounded a little like the chain of rationalizations that I'd wrapped around cheating my wife. If I was going to turn my back on this, I might as well just go to work fulltime up at Alec's.

One evening a few days later I jumped into the pickup and headed for Limestone Creek. The kamikaze approach. If I'd tried to make plans, I might have gotten discouraged. I did take one feeble precaution. I phoned my neighbor, John Minarik, and asked him to come over and feed Lewis if he didn't hear from me after a few days. I also took a thermos of coffee to keep me awake on the drive.

All was peaceful when I arrived at the foot of the canyon, but then it was four o'clock in the morning. I parked my truck well down the road and tiptoed into the woods, feeling fairly clever. But I knew I was in trouble an hour or so later when the dawn light revealed a beer can twinkling in the creek. It hadn't been there the previous trip, nor the cigarette ends and candy wrappers I found farther upstream. I find it depressing to follow a trail of such things into a place like Limestone Canyon. I also found it unnerving in this case, but I kept going, past Vibram boot marks in the sandbars.

I found out who'd preceded me where the creek forked into steeper, narrower beds. I hadn't expected it to be an old enemy.

"Here he is, Piss-fir Willy himself. His very own self. Except you're not a piss-fir anymore, are you, Kilgore? You're just one of us low-down private businessmen, right?"

"That's right."

"So we shouldn't be hearing any orders, eh?" Don Knudsen spoke with the slightly stiff, singsong intonation that people from the backwoods up here sometimes have. I'm not sure where it comes from, maybe from the Scandinavian or Indian background. Knudsen was a black-haired, white-skinned little man, stocky, a little paunchy, but with a small man's impressive vitality and a professional logger's impressive muscles. He was a logger out of Willow Creek, and not a very reputable one. We really earned our salaries keeping an eye on him when he got a contract. He was inclined to run over sale boundaries, cut seed and marker trees, or haul away loads of uncontracted hardwood to sell as firewood at two hundred bucks a cord in San Francisco. His equipment was the oldest and worst, and if it suffered terminal breakdown in the woods, he'd strip it and leave it, along with other sordid relics of his presence, junk piles, makeshift latrines, poached deer or bear bones.

There was a story that Knudsen had put a down payment on a piece of old-growth forest owned by a widow in Mendocino, had clear-cut it, and then had defaulted on the loan, leaving the widow a couple of thousand dollars richer and a lot wiser. From what I knew of him, he probably hadn't done it with premeditation. He was a poor man with rich appetites. He'd probably bought the place with dreams of becoming a land baron, then spent all the clear-cut profits on his other debts, leaving nothing left over for the loan payments on the widow's land.

85

There were three other men with Knudsen: one small, paunchy, and white faced, a brother probably; the other two, postadolescent and goonish, with big fatty muscles under pimpled skin. They seemed to be waiting for me to comment, so I obliged.

"Pretty strenuous walk up here." One of the postadolescents guffawed.

"Ooo, stwenuous," said the other.

"Sure is," said Knudsen. "Why'd you bother coming all the way up here?"

"I might ask you the same thing."

"It might be none of your damned business. You might not have a right to be asking people what they're doing in these woods. I'll tell you something. If there's anybody has a right to be asking people what they're doing in these woods, it's not you; it's me. I was born right down at the mouth of this canyon. So what do you think you're doing in my woods?"

"Right on," said the postadolescent who could talk. The other one guffawed again.

"I thought they were Pierre Grenville's woods." Knudsen ignored that. He was pumping himself up, visibly swelling.

"You think you're goddamned smart, don't you? You think you're the only one knows what's going on in these woods? I've been walking up and down this creek for forty-two years. This creek drowned my little sister in 1964; tore our house apart like it was a logjam. You know all these pretty pools up along here? Ain't a damned one of them wasn't full of sand after those floods. I know what the hell lives in this creek."

While he talked, I sidled up the bank and looked behind them. They'd made a camp: tents, backpacks, rifles, nothing unusual— except some snorkeling equipment and two small metal drums, the kind they pack pesticides in. One of the postadolescents began gravitating toward me.

If Limestone Creek was dammed, its old-growth forest would be logged first, and Knudsen would love a job where he could

86

take *all* the trees. It was obvious that the finding of a new species of vertebrate in the creek would make it hard to dam. That somebody might actually poison the whole creek to prevent that hadn't seriously occurred to me. I fended off the postadolescent and took a good look at the drums. Rotenone: Use only as directed.

The other postadolescent came over, and we went around and around for a while, but their muscles had the resilience of youth, and I wound up stuck between them. Knudsen ambled over and kicked me in the stomach.

"I've wanted to do that to a piss-fir for the longest time," he said. "Feels so good I think I'll do it again." He did, and I lost my lunch, splashing his shoes. It calmed him down: sea cucumbers have the right idea. When I got my breath back, I said I'd tell the law.

"Maybe you won't tell nobody. Maybe we'll leave you in one of these pools, let the steelheads chew on you."

"They don't feed while they're in the river."

"You can tell the law what you like, creep. They won't find anything here. Why should they listen to you? Everybody knows you're just a goddamned marijuana grower. They oughta put you in jail."

"You're going to wipe out a species just so you can log this place? Did Grenville put you up to this?"

"Who said wipe out? You think you're the only one cares about wildlife? I'll show you something. Bring him over here." They dragged me to a pool a little upstream in which a wire cage was submerged. Knudsen pulled it to shore. There were a half-dozen blue salamanders in it. "We ain't wiping them out. They're going where they belong, to zoos and places like that. They sure as hell don't belong in this creek, my friend, as you well know, you goddamned phony fraud."

"You think *I* put them in the creek?"

"You and your phony fraud environmentalist friends."

"Did you kill Blackwell?"

87

"I didn't kill nobody. But I might if you don't get the hell out of my sight. Are you going to leave, or are you going to try breathing underwater?"

"I'll leave."

"You got thirty seconds." He picked up a rifle and started counting. I managed to get out of range without too-undignified haste. Then I stopped, but the postadolescents were following, so I started again. They kept after me for about an hour. When they turned back, I stopped again, until I started seeing dace and suckers floating belly-up downstream. Then I went home.

Chapter Twelve

I PULLED OVER and slept awhile during the drive back, so I didn't get home until around nine the next morning. I half expected the barn to have burned down, but everything was undisturbed. Lewis ran out from under the porch, starving despite the dry food still in his dish. To shut him up, I gave him some of the expensive canned food he insists on. If I give him cheap canned food, he sniffs it, then makes scratching movements around it with his forepaws, the same as when he's burying his feces in the garden.

I went to bed and slept until evening, waking up in darkness with a bad taste in my mouth and a worse pain in my abdomen. Until they're bruised, you don't realize how important those abdominal muscles are for little things like standing, sitting, or walking. I stooped around the kitchen, wondering if I was herniated, if I'd have to wear a truss. I managed to make some eggs and tea and was pleased that my stomach accepted the offering. Lewis kept trying to climb into my lap, as insensitive to my discomforts as I am to his.

I turned on the news, half hoping for an outcry against a fish kill at Limestone Creek. It was the usual stuff: crime at the local level, taxes at the state level, unemployment at the national level, terrorism at the international level, sports and weather at the cosmic level. I was lucky enough not to be in the news myself, but then it would have taken longer than a day for the media to sniff out my remains if Knudsen had carried out his threats. It would have been easy for him to make sure that they never found me, which made me doubt, when I thought about it, that Knudsen could have killed Blackwell. Why do it in Oakland when he could have done it in Limestone Canyon?

I didn't like it, but I found myself believing most of what Knudsen had said. His remarks about the 1964 flood had made sense. Most of the canyons in northwestern California were torn apart by that flood. It seemed unlikely that an extremely rare species, apparently confined to a single canyon, could have survived it, not to mention all the other floods that have been tearing canyons apart since the Trinity Alps started rising over two million years ago. In all likelihood, Knudsen was right. Blackwell, or somebody, had planted the creatures.

It might have been a good idea if it had worked. Herpetologist discovers unknown species at proposed damsite. Make a reputation and stop a dam: really put one over on the bastards. It was the kind of thing I might have tried. I felt half responsible.

We grew up in the suburbs, Blackwell and I. Very normal, but it's a strange environment when you think about it. A deeply divided environment. Lots of nature there: trees, lawns, gardens, leftover bits of woodlot and farmland. You can get to love nature more easily than in the city, maybe even more easily than in the country, where you get the barnyard along with the greenery. Where Blackwell and I lived, there were backyard glimpses of pheasants and raccoons, and grouse and trout at a reservoir nearby. Nature seemed a paradise, especially when the alternative to running around in the woods was homework and dancing school. But it was a paradise that constantly disappeared as this floodplain got bulldozed for a parking lot and that woodlot got dug out for an office building.

Suburbs seem peaceful, but they are ecologically violent places as the old farm and woodland world is buried by the new home and lawn one. Children are sensitive to the violence and affected by it. They express it in various ways. There are the enemies of nature, who cut trees, kill birds and squirrels, and set up concentration camps and torture chambers for any hapless creature, from bug to toddler, that falls into their hands. There are the enemies of civilization, who destroy established artifacts like streetlights and windows. There are the enemies of progress, who haunt construction sites, good sources of things to smash and steal.

Blackwell and I belonged to one of the little packs that roamed around practicing all of the above categories of violence as occasion arose. We didn't think of ourselves as vandals or delinquents: everybody did it. More than the other pack members, we gravitated toward a swampy little ravine that the developers hadn't gotten to. Blackwell's amphibian obsession had surfaced, and there were plenty of bullfrogs, spring peepers, leopard frogs, and red-backed salamanders. I was more taken with the green herons, pileated woodpeckers, and kingfishers, but not averse to a little frog hunting.

There was an old pasture, grown to sumac and goldenrod, above the ravine. One autumn afternoon we saw a pair of does there, the first wild deer either of us had seen. It was like discovering a continent. When we returned to that pasture the next week, it was a soggy stretch of brown clay with a large yellow earth mover squatting in the middle. A school was to be built there, and Blackwell and I would spend our fifth and sixth grades in it.

Neither of us said a word as we slogged across the mud to that earth mover. We climbed up and peered into the glassed-in cab and sat awhile on the yellow painted steel. Then I began tentatively pounding a heel against the windshield. Blackwell jumped down, found a rock, and threw it against the glass. It hardly made a mark—tough glass—and bounced near my head.

"Hey, watch it," I said. Then I jumped down too, and we both started throwing stones against the glass, harder and harder, until we were throwing with all our might. The glass was tough, but we smashed it. We got into the cab and started ripping out anything breakable. Blackwell slashed the seat with his jack-

91

knife. We tried to burn the upholstery, then thought of dropping a match into the gas tank, but the cap was locked. Then we began to get nervous. We'd gone farther than normal vandalism: we'd broken into something. That was crime: we could go to reform school or military school. We got out of there.

I think that was an end of innocence for both of us. Childhood violence is innocent in that it's unknowing, undirected, no more deliberate in its way than a tree falling on a house. It's anger as a natural force. But Blackwell and I had realized what we were mad at, and our violence had become directed and thus predict-able, something that might be investigated and punished by the suburb-making world. We'd become responsible, probably for the first time in our lives.

A funny kind of responsibility, you might say. I'd hate to think of some kids doing that to my pickup. But we were defending something precious, whether pointlessly or not. After you do something like that, you never relate to the world in quite the same unfocused way that you did before. There's always that formative burst of anger back there. You're like a river that's cut itself a new channel during a flood.

Anger is like water, the way it sinks out of sight and then rises again unexpectedly. I didn't get angry at Knudsen until the next morning when I'd started to feel a little better. I began having blinding little visions of kicking *Knudsen* in the stomach, of force-feeding him a couple gallons of rotenone and *then* kicking him in the stomach. I went and jumped in the river to cool myself off.

I swam around awhile and felt a little calmer. It's hard to take yourself too seriously while minnows are nibbling your toes. Aside from the languorous deaths of Knudsen and his goons, what were my options? I could go to the sheriff and make a for-mal assault complaint, maybe accuse Knudsen of burglarizing my barn. That would be sensible. If I'd gone to Limestone Can-yon with some deputies instead of alone, the creek never would have been poisoned. I didn't like to think about that.

Thinking was painful, so I rationalized instead. The horse was already out of the barn, no use closing the door. Going to the sheriff now wouldn't accomplish much. The creek *was* poisoned, and I had no witnesses to it except Knudsen and his goons. I didn't see Knudsen as the basic problem anyway. I couldn't see him killing somebody over a few rare salamanders. If he'd stumbled on Blackwell planting them, he might have blown him away in a rage, but he wouldn't have traveled all the way to Oakland to do it. There was something else going on.

What that was, I had no idea. I thought of going and asking Pierre Grenville about it, but I doubted I'd get any better reception than I had from Knudsen, and Grenville lived in Arizona or someplace anyway. The only other option I could think of was talking to Blackwell's girlfriend, this Carla Shreve person.

I checked my mailbox on the way back from the river, hoping for a note from Dr. Todd about her address. The box yielded two shopper's gazettes, an electricity bill, a car-insurance bill, and direct-mail appeals to save sea turtles, African wildlife, liberalism, and international democracy. There was one from the Limestone Canyon Defense Council too. I sent off a check for that one. If I really wanted to justify my existence, I'd live on textured vegetable protein and answer every appeal with a fifty-dollar check. How many appeals a day would I get then? Maybe I could heat the trailer with them in winter, thus freeing my firewood budget for more contributions.

No note from Dr. Todd. I phoned him: he was out. From sheer frustration I phoned Grunewald, who laughed when I asked if there'd been any progress on Blackwell's case, thus suppressing any feeble desire I might have had to tell him my troubles. I said goodby hastily, before he could start interrogating me again. He was too good at that.

There were always seeds to plant, beds to water, weeds to pull. Humanity might find happiness if it would just accept and rejoice in the need to pull weeds and stop trying to get around it with cultivators and herbicides. After all, we evolved to scurry around picking up little things with our clever fingers and putting them in our clever mouths. Think of the peace that would descend on the planet if all five billion of us had to spend at least four hours a day pulling weeds and picking bugs off the tomatoes.

Chapter Thirteen

AFTER A COUPLE of days, I began to yearn for higher things than weeds and seeds. The only higher thing I could think of offhand was a trip to a bar in Weaverville. There are two bars in town: one, usually full, for cowboys and loggers; the other, usually empty, for everybody else. I went to the cowboy and logger bar, hoping for a little noise.

It was noisy, though not particularly full. Two cowboys were playing dice at the bar, and the jukebox was going full blast. Twang, moan, bleat. I like country music well enough, but when they play it even in grocery stores, it gets to be a bit much.

"Didn't think you used this stuff anymore," said the owner as he poured me a double bourbon. He remembered me from the Forest Service days, when we'd come in for a beer after a dusty day on the logging roads. I let that pass and gave him his money. I took a glance around, my eyes getting used to the gloom of the place, and saw Jimmy and Rodrigo sitting in the booth at the far end of the room.

Jimmy looked up and saw me, or looked at me. He seemed fairly drunk, with that fixed look in his eyes that somehow is more noticeable in drunken Indians than in drunken whites. I smiled and waved, thinking it might be just as well to stay where I was. But Jimmy beckoned, and Rodrigo turned his intense gaze on me too. Never snub a drunk. I took my glass over to their booth.

"Hey, man, have a seat." Jimmy waved me into the seat across from him, where Rodrigo leaned against the wall, staring straight ahead now. Even against the wall, he took up most of the seat. I eased myself in next to him. They were drinking what looked like rum and coke. "How you like that Alec, huh?"

"How do I like him?"

"Yeah, how do you like him?"

"Seems a little moody." Jimmy snorted. He said something to Rodrigo, and Rodrigo snorted. They both looked at me with a kind of amused curiosity that made my ears hot.

"Why are you looking like that?"

"Like what, man?"

"What is he, gay or something?"

Jimmy laughed and said something else to Rodrigo, who laughed and shifted around in his seat so that the glasses sloshed and tinkled on the tabletop.

"No, man, he's not gay. That is one thing Alec is *not*. You disappointed?"

"Mm."

"You gonna run his ranch for him?"

"Don't *you* want to?"

"You heard what he said. We're illegals. He wants a nice gringo boy, like you."

"Worked for Alec long?"

"Long time."

"In Guatemala too?"

"Oh yeah." The question bored him. He sat with his head slightly tilted back and seemed about to doze off.

"Why'd you leave?"

"Leave what?"

"Guatemala."

"Bad place now, man. Too many enemies." He opened his eyes wide again. "Hey, I'm not spending another winter in this place, though. Those winter nights, man. Too long and cold. Nothing alive out there."

"There's always Bigfoot."

"Big what?"

"Eight-foot-tall ape creatures that walk like men and whistle like owls."

"Don't bust my balls, man."

Rodrigo said something.

"What'd he say?"

"He says he likes the snow. His mother was Polish, so he thinks maybe he's an Eskimo or something. Kill a polar bear with a knife."

"I thought he didn't understand English."

"He knows a few words."

"Thinking of going back south?"

"Could be, man."

"Alec still do business down there?"

"Could be."

"Alec run much coke?"

"Are you kidding me? Hey, don't mess with Alec." He made a chopping motion with his hand. It seemed to irritate Rodrigo. They talked heatedly for a moment. Jimmy made the chopping motion again. "You get the *dolor* instead of the dollar."

"*Dolor?*"

"Grief, man. You get the grief."

"What kind of grief?"

"Don't ask. Have another drink."

We had another drink. Conversation lagged. There was the same tension between Rodrigo and Jimmy that I'd sensed before: contempt on Jimmy's part and a kind of mulish hostility on Rodrigo's. They were like a pair of tourists who'd been traveling together so long that they'd come to detest each other but who were still bound together by their foreignness.

"Do you think I should run Alec's ranch?"

"It's your ass."

97

"My ass if I do or my ass if I don't?"

"It's just your ass."

"That sounds like a truism."

"Your ass especially when you're using those fancy words."

"You don't care for them?"

"It's not what I care, man; it's that you aren't as smart as you think. Alec's smarter than you."

"How do you know?"

"Because he's smarter than me, and you're not."

"Want to fight?"

Jimmy's face broke into a smile of surprising sweetness. He wagged a finger at me. "Ah-ah-ah. Hey, I like you, man," he said. "Just sharing my thoughts with you, you know? No harm intended."

I was easily mollified. My abdomen was still sore. In fact, I'd scared myself. I decided it was time to go home. Jimmy and Rodrigo were being served another rum and coke as I left. They looked ready to spend the night there, glowering at each other. I suppose it was a relief from chaperoning Dobermans and coyotes.

I didn't know quite what to make of Jimmy's warning. The obvious explanation was that he was jealous of Alec's offer to me, however casual or frivolous, and wanted to scare me off. It didn't feel like that, though; I didn't sense any real resentment in Jimmy. There was something detached about him.

I decided it would be a good idea to be very straight and aboveboard with Alec: do the plan, have him approve it, plant the trees, and goodby. I got out my maps and calculator again and started racking my brains. It takes a lot of paperwork to plan a commercial forest. It's like planning a war: a matter of getting healthy troops (in this case trees) to the right places at the right times. That's more or less the boring part. But there's something godlike about it too. I think about all the trees that I've put in the ground, slowly growing, all those extensions of George. It's a nice ego trip, but there's something more to it. Americans love to build, but they don't do enough maintenance. I felt that I was doing some maintenance. When you create something, you destroy something. When you maintain something, you don't destroy.

I still couldn't get Blackwell's girlfriend out of my mind. I called Todd again; he was out of town. It had occurred to me that if Blackwell had planted the creatures in Limestone Creek, he must have discovered them somewhere else, or gotten them from somebody who'd discovered them somewhere else. Todd had told me that Carla Shreve had discovered an unknown species of salamander in Latin America somewhere. Had Blackwell planted some of those in Limestone Creek? That wouldn't have made much sense. They'd have liked the Trinity Alps winter even less than Jimmy did.

Two days later I finally got Dr. Todd on the phone. He'd been at a conference. I told him I'd been back to Limestone Creek and returned empty-handed. I left out the other details; they were too embarrassing.

"You never found out who stole your specimen?"

"No." I wasn't exactly lying. Knudsen hadn't admitted stealing it.

"Curious business. But salamanders can be hard to find."

"Did you ever find that woman herpetologist's address? Carla Shreve?"

"Oh, I'm sorry. I did. It's not an address exactly. Now where is it?" Shuffling papers. "Ah. Post office box 297, Cave Junction, Oregon 97523."

"Cave Junction."

"Isn't that near you?"

"Give or take a few hundred miles. How old is the address?"

"I suppose it's been a few years."

"How did she come to work for the museum?"

"I think Tom recommended her, actually. I think she was a student of his."

"They were friends?"

"Hm. She did a good job for us. I'm not prepared to comment on their personal relationship."

99

"Did they go on field trips together?"

"Not under the museum's auspices. She was doing cataloging and classification work."

"Tom told me he'd been to Latin America on collecting trips."

"He may have on his vacations. Not for us; we don't have any Latin American collections."

"This salamander Carla Shreve discovered. Did you ever see a specimen?"

"I think she showed me a slide."

"It wasn't blue?"

"Oh, no, it was a little gray and yellow lungless salamander. A plethodontid. They're always discovering new species because that type of salamander spends most of its life underground." A pause. "Are you suggesting that Tom might have *planted* that salamander?"

"It's a possibility." I told him about the flood. I'd already told him about the dam controversy.

"But he must have discovered it somewhere."

"I suppose so. Or taken one from somebody who had discovered it. Was he capable of doing something like that?"

"In effect, of perpetrating a hoax to enhance his professional reputation?"

"Yes."

"Well, it needed some enhancement. But you could say that of a lot of herpetologists. Or ornithologists. Or entomologists. They aren't exactly glamour fields."

"Might have been a publicity boost for the museum."

"To have one of our staff caught perpetrating a hoax?" He chose to ignore my insinuation. Not a very nice insinuation and not a very likely one from what I'd seen of Dr. Todd.

"I guess not."

"If you see Carla, tell her hello for us."

Chapter Fourteen

I THOUGHT OF WRITING Carla Shreve a letter but decided it would be better to talk to her in person. She wasn't in the Illinois Valley phone book. If she had a post office box in a little place like Cave Junction, she'd probably be pretty easy to locate. It was a long day's drive up there, but I was getting used to long day's drives. I was getting pretty curious about her. But first I finished the reforestation plan.

Alec Rice didn't seem overjoyed when I phoned to tell him the good news. He said he might be able to look at the plan if I brought it up right away: he was leaving on a trip tomorrow. I was getting a little tired of his hot and cold running charm, but I said I'd be up right away. Kilgore's same-day service. Maybe I should wear a little uniform and a bow tie.

The gate to his private road was locked when I got there. I sat and wondered if I should turn around and go home or gather up my papers and start walking. Or maybe start crawling on my belly? It would be a couple of hours' walk, but then that check had been good as gold. Fortunately Rodrigo came roaring down in the big pickup and opened the gate for me. I drove through smiling and waving like an idiot to his stolid impassivity. In the rearview mirror I could see him closing it again as I pulled away.

Alec received me in a study off the living room. It contained a small computer, a video terminal, and a photocopier, among

101

other things. I could hear somebody moving around in another part of the house: probably Wendy packing. Jimmy wasn't in evidence. Alec listened impassively to the plan. He nodded. Then he pointed to the map I'd laid out on his table.

"Okay," he said. "I want those five areas deleted." He was pointing to the five best timber-growing areas in the plan. I told him that. He shrugged.

"That'll change the estimate quite a bit."

"That's all right." For *him* it was all right.

"Why do you want to delete them?"

"I need them for something else."

"Grazing cattle?"

"No." The subject evidently wasn't open to discussion.

"If you say so."

Alec's response to that concession was to stick his nose into my labor-cost estimates. "I'll supply the labor for planting the trees," he said.

"What? You never said that. I got a regular crew I work with. It's almost a union contract, for God's sake. They'll quit if they find out I hired other people."

"You won't hire them. It won't cost you anything."

"But I'll have to change the estimate for that too."

"Pay yourself for the extra time. Anybody who works up here, I employ."

"What if I brought them up? You could talk to them."

"I don't owe anybody any explanations."

I'd already spent part of Alec's money, but I could give back the rest. "All right," I said, "I'll sell you the plan and seedlings, and you can plant them yourself."

"Uh-uh. I want you to supervise it. I want a professional job."

"Sorry, I don't like these conditions."

Alec turned red. He stood up abruptly and walked out of the room. He was gone for a good twenty minutes, which first bemused, then annoyed, me. Then I began to get nervous. I went into the living room and listened. There wasn't a sound in the house, which made me think of my overnight visit. I pictured

Alec and Wendy lying in coffins in the basement with blood on their chins. But these old ranch houses don't have basements.

Alec came back and sat down, looking normal. "Where were we?"

"Labor relations?"

The phone rang. Alec picked it up and listened a minute, then put it back on the receiver. Then he picked it up again, rather absentmindedly, and smashed a glass on his desk with it. He didn't do it violently, just kept tapping the glass (a tumbler, actually) a little harder each time until it was in pieces. Then he put the phone on the receiver again. He began picking up shards of the glass and lobbing them into a wastebasket across the room.

"You think your friends wouldn't go to work for somebody else who offered them more money than you?" Crash. Tinkle.

"Not if they didn't like him."

"Power comes from popularity?"

"Sometimes."

He stopped throwing glass and leaned back in his chair. "It's the other way around, George. Always."

"You're popular?"

"I could be. Right now I have other interests."

"Planning to automate?"

"Always more people, and always less use for them. What does that say to you?"

"Not much. Misplaced priorities."

"Actually, in the end you want a labor force that's more responsive than a machine."

"Popularity."

"You see? We're basically in agreement." He swept the remaining glass onto the floor, leaving it for his labor force to pick up. "We'll talk about this later. I'm in a kind of a rush."

"Okay, but I still don't like the conditions."

"We'll work something out." He smiled. His teeth weren't particularly sharp, but they were very white. Probably capped. He picked up the phone again and started to dial.

"When will you be back?" I asked.

103

"I'll call you."

When I was halfway there I remembered about seeing Rodrigo close the gate. I kept going, hoping that he hadn't locked it. He had. I waited awhile. It was impossible to drive around it. I went back to the ranch headquarters. Rodrigo came out of a barn very fast as I drove up. He relaxed when he saw it was me, but he didn't give me a kiss. I tried to think of something Spanish for gate.

"*El porto.*" I made opening motions.

He nodded. "*Barrera.*"

"Whatever. Open her up, okay?"

He looked at me awhile, then went into the house. He was in there much longer than I liked, but he finally emerged, jumped in the pickup, and roared off.

He was holding the gate open when I caught up. I liked him a little better, so I paused a moment.

"Where's Jimmy?" No response. "*Su amigo?*" He shrugged. I couldn't think of anything else to say, so I drove away.

I found out where Jimmy was that evening. He phoned me from Redding.

"Hey, I'm getting out of this place," he said.

"Well, uh, have a nice trip."

"The thing is, I need some traveling money, you know?"

"Traveling money?"

"I thought you might be able to loan me a little."

"Didn't Alec pay you?"

"Alec and I are not speaking."

"Yeah, but still—."

"Hey, forget about Alec."

"You know, really, I have cash flow problems right now."

"A couple hundred dollars. I'll tell you something that will interest you. Something you should know."

"About what?"

"About Alec."

"How am I supposed to *get* this money to you if you're in Redding?"

"Bring it down here tomorrow."

"Oh yeah? Anything else I can do?"

"Look, man, I wouldn't ask if I didn't need this. You seemed like good people."

"What is this you're going to tell me?"

"I can't say now."

"Give me a hint."

"No, man. Meet me at the Casa Sinaloa restaurant on Oak Street at noon tomorrow. Make sure Rodrigo's not following you."

"I don't like the sound of this."

"You'll like it even less if you don't hear what I have to tell you, believe it."

"I'd have to go to the bank."

"Bank opens at ten. Take you an hour to get here."

"I don't like it."

"All right, the hell with you."

"No—. I'll come."

Redding baked under a photochemical haze. There are some nice back streets in Redding, but the downtown has to be one of the ugliest in the valley. You'd think they'd go in for shade trees, considering the heat, but air-conditioning is easier than raking leaves or trimming branches. The Casa Sinaloa had a big cottonwood beside it, but then it wasn't in the classiest part of town.

It had air-conditioning too and dim lighting and squeaky leatherette booths. I sat down in one and told the waitress I was expecting a friend. Jimmy showed up fifteen minutes later.

"Sorry to keep you waiting."

"Always glad to visit Redding."

"Have some lunch. Pretty good food, for Mexicans."

"Am I paying for that too?"

"My treat. Have the carne asada."

I had the carne asada, which was good.

Jimmy eyed me speculatively. I asked him what he saw.

"Hey, I'm not looking at anything."

"Hm." I took two hundred dollars out of my wallet and placed it in front of him. He slipped it into his pocket with hardly a glance. "Where you going?"

"Where am I going? South, man, south."

"You and Alec had a falling out?"

Jimmy snorted, and a look of surprising unhappiness passed for a moment over his face, which usually was set in a cheerfully sardonic expression. "Yeah," he said. "What do you know about Alec?"

"I thought you were going to tell *me* about Alec."

"I am. Be a little patient."

"He has a lot of money, which he probably made from drugs."

"Yeah, but what do you *know* about him? What does he seem like to you?"

"I've hardly met the guy, for God's sake. I don't know. An egomaniac. A bully. Smart."

Jimmy glanced around the room, which was fairly full and noisy, and leaned closer to me over the table. It was a little embarrassing. Melodramatic. "You think he could have killed hundreds of people?" he said.

"What?"

Jimmy leaned back in his seat again, as though experiencing some kind of release.

"What do you mean?" I said.

"You weren't expecting me to say that, were you?" He was right: I hadn't been expecting him to say that. I'd thought he was going to tell me something useful about Alec's dope connections. "I can read you, man. You're wondering what it has to do with you."

"What does it have to do with me?"

"Know your employer, man."

"What people?"

Jimmy leaned forward again eagerly. He wasn't eating much. He lowered his voice, but it got more intense as it got lower, so that I was surprised everybody in the restaurant wasn't turning their heads. But they just kept eating and babbling away.

106

"Refugees, man. From Guatemala, El Salvador, Nicaragua. They paid Alec to take them across the border, and he killed them. Men, women, and children."

"How do you know this?"

"There's no trace of them in the States. Their friends, relatives never heard from them again."

"What are you, some kind of agent?"

Jimmy didn't say anything.

"Why would Alec kill refugees?"

"Maybe for their money. Maybe somebody paid him to. I don't know, man."

"Then how do you know he killed them?"

"Rodrigo talks."

"And you listen. And Rodrigo tells Alec you listen."

"Something like that."

"Shit."

"Rodrigo had a good time. Young women. Girls."

"Why the hell are you telling me this?"

"I thought you should know. I thought somebody should know what those bastards did."

"You said you worked for Alec for a long time."

"Too goddamned long. I didn't believe it myself until Rodrigo told me."

"I don't know if I should believe *you*."

"You don't want to, do you?"

"Alec doesn't need to murder people for money."

"Who said he needs to? People like him never get enough money. Alec argues over change in restaurants."

"Yeah, but what could he get from refugees?"

Jimmy shook his head, impatient. "I don't know, man. What difference does it make? Maybe he collects the heads."

"What?" I put my fork down.

"Hey, don't lose your lunch. I'm paying good money for it."

"My money."

"Relax, man."

"You're telling me Alec has a roomful of heads somewhere?"

107

"Don't be so literal. It's just speculation."

"This is insane."

"It's a power trip for him maybe, like killing sharks. Except with Rodrigo it's a body trip, and with Alec it's a head trip. He likes to get your mind, you know?"

"No, I don't know."

"I think you do know, man."

"Maybe nobody was killed. Maybe Rodrigo was busting your balls."

"Oh yeah, he'd bust my balls all right. You must be a little stupid, man. You think it's not easy? Along the border? Easier all the time, man. The more people, the easier to kill." Jimmy had been leaning across the table again. He sat back and rubbed his nose. "You heard the coyotes up there, right?"

"At his place? Yeah."

"Last summer Alec was staying there, decided the coyotes were keeping him awake. So he calls up this friend of his, and a couple of days later a guy shows up in a panel truck. Man, you've never seen so many ways to kill coyotes as he had in that truck: traps, poison. The guy looked like he ate poison for breakfast: he was this funny color, metallic like.

"So Alec and this guy go to work. Alec wasn't just hiring the guy to kill coyotes for him; he was into it. They even tried shooting them from helicopters, but there was too much cover. He had the whole side of that barn covered with dead coyotes, not just coyotes. I never would have known there were so many animals up there. He took all the skins and sold them too. He would have fed the rest to his dogs if it wasn't full of poison."

"Lots of coyotes up there now."

"Sure there are, man."

"I'm not calling you a liar."

"Hey, man, I don't *care* what you call me. Just pay attention to what I've told you a little. Alec is a man who likes to kill."

"Why don't you kill *him*?"

"Did I say *Alec* would be easy to kill? And some people want to know more. Alec has connections down there. He may have

108

been doing people favors; that's another possibility. Your government doesn't like people disappearing in El Salvador, but if they disappear in Sonora, who cares? Just another wetback, right?"

"But you didn't find out."

"Fucking Alec is smart."

"I don't know what the hell I'm supposed to do about this." I didn't like the querulous tone in my voice.

"You're not supposed to do anything, man. Just watch your ass. Alec seems to like you for some reason. I'd be a little careful if Alec seemed to like me. Anyway, it's not your problem, is it? You want your money back?" My fingers itched, but self-esteem won over avarice.

"I said I'd give it to you."

"I'll pay it back. I've got your address."

"Where'd you get that?"

"The phone book."

"Oh. What did you do for Alec in Central America?"

"Lots of things."

"Did you ever run into a guy named Tom Blackwell, a biologist?"

"No, I didn't know anybody like that. I've got to go catch a bus now. Take it easy, man." Jimmy dropped some bills on the table and walked out.

Chapter Fifteen

WHAT DO YOU DO when somebody tells you your star client is a mass murderer? Give him his money back? Alec wasn't asking me to plant Hispanic leftists on his property, just trees. Go to the sheriff? Alec hadn't perpetrated any massacres on his ranch; otherwise Jimmy would have had evidence of it. Jimmy didn't have evidence of anything. It all seemed unreal. I did nothing for a couple of days.

I took a walk along the river on the second evening, wriggling my shoulders to get the cramp out. I was planting the last of the seeds. Business as usual. I skirted a willow thicket and saw Alec's truck parked on a gravel bar across the river. I didn't know of any other red, two-seater pickups in the vicinity. I didn't see who was in it, if anybody, but I didn't look very hard. The prospect of a chance meeting with Alec or Rodrigo beside the twilit river did not please me. Alec had said he was taking a trip, but he hadn't said where. I started back toward the trailer and decided it was time to go see Carla Shreve.

I stopped at my neighbor's on the way, to thank him for watching out for Lewis and to ask him to do it again. At least somebody would know if I disappeared forever. John Minarik was working hard in his garden, as usual. He had orchards, livestock, and a gold claim up near Denny too, a typical early retirement.

"Your garden looked a little peaked, so I watered it," he said.

"Thanks."

"Want me to water it while you're gone this time too?"

"I'd really appreciate that, John."

"No use planting them if you don't water them." John didn't really approve of my living alone and growing trees. He thought I should be down in Redding, sitting at a desk and paying into pension and college plans. And life insurance. Growing trees was something you did *after* retirement, after the real work of management was done. Maybe he was a little jealous: the nursery would have been a good outlet for his energies.

I gave Lewis the remains of some chicken I'd been gnawing on, loaded a backpack, and waited until it was quite dark. Then, just to be on the safe side, I drove out on a gravel road that looped behind my and Minarik's properties before meeting up with the main highway about a half mile west of my driveway entrance. I pulled over and slept awhile between Eureka and Crescent City and crossed the border just as it started getting light.

Driving up U.S. 199 into southern Oregon is weird. You're used to the lushness of the redwood coast and the Smith River drainage, so you want it to get even lusher as you pass into bucolic Oregon. The Illinois Valley through which the highway runs is closer to the coast than the Trinity Alps are. Instead of lushness, you get something a little like the deserts of the Modoc Plateau a hundred miles inland: rabbitbrush flats, straggling Jeffrey pines, creekbeds full of what look like rusty cannonballs.

Over this surprise desolation loom mountains with what look like acute cases of sunburn. They have a salmony pink tint like that of human skin when it's broiled and salted on a beach, and they're about as bare. The only vegetation visible on them from a distance is stunted conifers sticking out like isolated hairs. Just looking at those mountains makes your skin itch and burn.

The red peridotite of the mountains really is burned rock, but burned at much higher temperatures than any beach. It comes from sixty miles down in the earth's crust, which would be very fiery indeed if there were airspace for flames to live on down there. Although there's plenty of rainfall, peridotite is toxic to

111

most plants except a few conifers and some odd little shrubs and herbs. Needless to say, the peridotite country has been a disappointment to the Forest Service, which administers much of it. There are patches of good timber soil, but they're scattered and hard to reach, so a lot of the area is in the Kalmiopsis Wilderness Area and various botanical preserves.

I found the Cave Junction post office, but things got harder after that. Carla Shreve no longer had a box there; in fact, the young woman in the office didn't know of anybody named Carla Shreve or of a woman biologist in the area. That struck me as a little odd because the young woman seemed the type who would know about such things. She seemed hip—not hippy, but hip. It struck me as even odder by the afternoon, when I'd talked to a few people around town. Some of them knew of a woman biologist in the area, and a few even knew her name, or approximations of it. None of them seemed to know where she lived, except that it was in the hills.

It wasn't unusual for them not to know where Carla Shreve lived. It was unusual for the woman in the post office not to know of her very existence. Small mountain towns just don't work that way. Having nothing else to do by five o'clock, I lurked around the post office and watched the young woman take down the flag, lock the doors, get in a Datsun pickup, and drive away south on the highway.

I scurried into my truck, hoping the young woman wasn't being too observant, and followed her to the south end of the valley, where she left the highway on a gravel road heading west. I kept going on the highway in case she *was* being observant, pulled over and waited ten minutes, then went back to the gravel road and followed her. She was long gone: like many people who drive gravel a lot, she was driving it fast. I saw her dust ahead of me a few times. After the road had swung around a number of creek bends, I found the Datsun parked in front of a cabin.

I kept driving until the cabin was out of sight, then parked the truck and started walking back. A car door slammed, and I ducked behind a tree. I heard the car start, then recede in the direction of Cave Junction. When I came in sight of the cabin again, the young woman's Datsun was gone. Evidently it wasn't her place.

The cabin was built with its facade right on the road, as mountain cabins sometimes are when the slope is so steep that you'd have to do a half gainer in the front door if it was set back. But there was no door in the facade, as though the builder had had second thoughts about being so accessible from the road. There was a window, but I didn't want to get off to a bad start by peeping into it. I looked for a door. The cabin seemed to ramble down the slope on several levels, an early example of mine-shaft modern. There was one encouraging sign, a Land-Rover parked in a shed on the other side of the road.

I finally found a wooden ramp, concealed by live oaks, that led to a door in a lower level. I knocked, waited a minute, then knocked harder. A woman in a flannel shirt, dungarees, and hiking boots opened.

"Carla?"

She just looked at me.

"Carla Shreve?"

She didn't deny it.

I had envisioned a woman herpetologist as looking batrachian, which was sexist of me. Blackwell didn't look like a salamander. If this woman was like any cold-blooded creature, it was more like some colorful, sinuous snake, a racer or a whipsnake. Her eyes were a golden brown that you see more often in snakes than in humans. Her hair was the same color, and the small head on her long neck seemed as fine boned and delicate as a racer's, though there was nothing reptilian about her high forehead and pointed chin. Her arms, legs, and hands were so long and slender that they might have looked odd if they hadn't been so shapely. The rest of her was shapely too, a fact accentuated by the rough clothes she wore. She looked back into the house a moment, then turned to face me again.

"Do I know you?"

"No. You may know a friend of mine. Tom Blackwell?"

113

"I know Tom." The name didn't seem to be the key to her heart.

"Did you know he's been murdered?" I couldn't think of anything else to say. The words hung in the air, like gratuitous obscenities.

"What are you doing here?" She looked at me as though I might have murdered him, which took me aback.

"It's a long story. Could I come in?"

"I'm afraid I don't have time."

"Er—."

"No, I'm sorry." She began to close the door.

"I came all the way from California to talk to you."

"I'm sorry." The door shut and a bolt clicked.

"Hey! Come on." I started pounding on the door, but the cabin was as silent as if she'd never appeared. I began to feel foolish. I couldn't very well kick the door down. I had a feeling she was the kind who would resist more if she was pushed.

My only other option was to get in my truck and go home. As I was thinking of doing so, I again noticed the single window facing the road and peeped without hesitation. There were curtains drawn, but by craning my neck I could glimpse bare floorboards, part of a desk, and what looked like a backpack with a tent stuffsack strapped to it. It didn't seem like the kind of room one would store a backpack in.

I got in the pickup and, hoping Carla Shreve wasn't watching, headed west on the gravel road, away from 199. At the first opportunity I pulled off the road and hid the truck in some trees. If she *was* going backpacking, as seemed possible from her clothes and the pack, I had no way of knowing if she was heading in this direction, but it was better than nothing. I was tired of driving anyway.

I watched the road until dusk but saw no Land-Rover or Datsun pickup. My head ached, my skin was gritty, and my throat was dry. There didn't seem to be any running water around. I had some water in my bottle, enough to drink but not to cook with. I ate some cheese and crackers and dried fruit. A Douglas squirrel that was taking a sawdust bath on a punky log got annoyed at my presence, and its complaints attracted two Steller's jays and some chestnut-backed chickadees, who also disapproved. Shadowing somebody through the woods would have its problems, but I kept an eye out until it was quite dark. Then I lay down in the back of the truck and slept pretty well, except for the explorations of the local white-footed mouse. There's nothing a mouse likes better than a vehicle parked in the woods.

I awoke to the rumbling and popping of tires on gravel and made it in sight of the road just in time to see the back end of what *looked* like a Land-Rover disappearing around a curve. It wasn't too hard to follow the fresh tire tracks in the dust for about ten winding miles, which, trending southwest, must have carried me down near the California border. For the first five miles bits of styrofoam, straw, and lint kept flying out of one of my dashboard vents. The mouse had been building a nest in it. Mice no sooner find some new territory than they start to build on it: just like people. I wondered what the mouse thought of its new real estate's sudden disappearance. Probably vowed to rebuild bigger and better.

The tracks swung right, onto a jeep road that led back north toward the roadless country stretching forty miles to the Rogue River Canyon. The tracks were harder to see in the pine duff and bare rock of the jeep road, but there weren't many turnoffs. Even with four-wheel drive, I was apprehensive about some of the grades and mudholes I had to traverse. The peridotite country may seem dry, but it's full of little swamps that look like mere green spots on a hillside from a distance but turn out to be chest tall with lilies, coneflowers, azaleas, and the strange cobra plants with their insect-devouring hoods.

I found the Land-Rover parked about four miles up the jeep road, on a ridgeline so narrow that there barely was room to pull in and park behind it. It looked like Carla Shreve's Land-Rover, though I wasn't positive, not having had the brains to write down the license number. There was no sign of her or of any human presence except the jeep road and some clear-cut slopes to the south and west. There wasn't a sound. I'm a little un-nerved by the silence of such exposed places. You expect a red-wood canyon or cedar swamp to be silent, but to be able to see hundreds of square miles at the same time you hear nothing is weird. People wonder whether a tree falling in the forest would make a noise if nobody was there to hear it. What if somebody *was* there and it didn't make a noise?

Close examination turned up an unpromising trail leading northwest, with slender, smallish boot tracks on it. Unless you're walking on bare rock or heavy duff, it's impossible not to leave tracks when you're carrying a backpack. Carla's footprints would look like that. I broke out my gear and started in pursuit.

Hiking in the Kalmiopsis was different from hiking in the Trin-itys. In the Alps the sharp, glacier-carved peaks of the Salmon Trinity Crest dominate everything and provide a comforting sense of orientation. You have to spend two or three days of solid climbing to *get* to the crest, but it's always up there. Once you've reached it, you're on top of the place, so to speak. There's an order to it: you start in dusty oaks, work your way up through pine and fir, and end up in the mountain hemlocks around the high lakes. The Kalmiopsis doesn't have that kind of order; there's no real top to it. There are peaks all over the place, but they don't form a tidy spine or crest. If you climb one, you have to climb down into some canyon before you can climb the next. The vegetation follows the jigsaw puzzle of geology more than the neat zonation of altitude. Within a few hours I crept through heavy Douglas fir forest, stumbled over barrens of stunted pines and scorched red rock, dropped into a swamp so full of Port Orford cedar and mosquitoes that there was scarcely room to breathe, pushed through scratchy manzanita and cean-othus brush, and swung precariously along a steep, dusty can-yonside of live oak.

All this was interesting, but it would have been more so if I'd been in better shape. Observation is hard when your heart is bouncing like an overinflated basketball. There's nothing like a little backpacking to remind you that aging begins at twenty-one. I decided I must have lost a lot of brain cells because it took me awhile to notice that I hadn't seen any smallish, slender boot tracks on the trail for a long time.

I backtracked—up and down, up and down—until I found one again. There was impenetrable brush on both sides of the trail, so I turned around again and walked along to a canyon bottom that seemed a likely place for Carla to have turned aside. I couldn't find any boot tracks in the creekbed sand, but she could have been walking on stones so as not to leave a trail.

It wasn't as easy a canyon to follow as Limestone Canyon. It was very V-shaped, with logjams, red boulders big as houses, landslides, willow thickets, sheer cliffs, and piles of big river stones that made ankle-twisting shifts under almost every foot-step. But I kept going, deeper and deeper.

People talk about the "lure of the wild," referring vaguely to clean air, spring water, mountain greenery, and so on, but there's an allurement to wild country that can be less benign. It pulls you in. There's something almost hypnotic about it. The con-scious source of the attraction can be almost anything—a pret-tier campsite, a bigger buck, gold, simple curiosity—but you build up a kind of compelling rhythm that underlies conscious desire. You feel that there will be more of what attracts you beyond the next ridge or bend in the creek, so you go on to that, and then you want to see what's beyond the *next*, and so on, while the sun gets a little lower and the trail back a little fainter. You can turn around, with the sense of defeat that entails, or you can go on, until the trail is lost and the sun is down.

So I found myself, about 10:00 P.M., when the last semipre-cious tint had faded from the sky and I no longer could see the rocks I was stepping on. But nature is merciful: it allows life without trails, for a while. I laid out my sleeping bag on a sand-bar, ate some cheese and crackers, and listened to the creek. I was tired enough to have no awareness of falling asleep. Con-sciousness simply stopped.

117

Chapter Sixteen

I AM ALWAYS STRUCK by the constriction of civilized life after returning from a place like the Kalmiopsis. It's physical as well as mental. Familiar rooms seem ridiculously small: walking into them is like putting on a shrunken undershirt. The psyche expands to fill available space. Emotions get bigger, which is not always a source of gladness.

Watching night fall on a place from which you're not sure how to get back can make you want to curl up in a ball and weep. On the other hand, the sunrise after such a night can make you want to shout for joy, and not just at having survived the night. You can want to get even *more* lost. It's a hard joy to analyze. It probably has to do with physical movement, which is so channeled and constrained by civilization that the prospect of simply following your nose for a day can be intoxicating.

Of course, the Kalmiopsis placed its own constraints on my movement. Several times as I crept up the narrowing and steepening canyon, it seemed about to *stop* movement. But I wormed my way along. About mid-morning, I got to the inevitable fork. I still hadn't seen any boot tracks. I arbitrarily chose the left fork and followed it, but it became impassable about an hour later. One route she probably hadn't followed. I backtracked to the right fork, which was just about as steep and brushy but which had more forest on its slopes, so that I was able to pull myself along through the trees until the slope grew gentler near the ridgetop where the canyon headed.

The view from the ridgetop was nice but unenlightening. My map said there was a ridgetop trail in the vicinity, but I didn't see one. I followed the ridge north for a while, but it started to dip into another canyon. I didn't want to go into another canyon, especially not through the jumble of brush and boulders on the slope. I backtracked, looking for connections with other north-trending ridges, didn't find any, and finally settled for climbing down a gentle, forested slope. After about a quarter of a mile, it turned into a giant's staircase of red cliffs. I tried moving parallel to the cliffs but soon came to a gully so steep that I had to follow it back to the ridgetop.

The Kalmiopsis had me running in circles, which you shouldn't let a wilderness do to you. The sun was getting low again, and I was out of water. I bowed to the inevitable and followed the ridgeline down the brushy slope I'd tried to avoid. It was easier than it looked (did I imagine the remnants of a path?), and there was water at the bottom. It was already pretty dim down there, and I decided it was time for a cooked meal.

I had bad dreams that night. Not the kind in which monsters chase you. I'd have preferred that kind because you feel good when they're over. These dreams lingered at the back of my throat the next morning: a sluggish stream of repulsive images—vivisected flesh; limbs skewered on steel rods or turned on lathes, peeling off glistening rolls of skin, muscle, and fat. Sun and fatigue can do disagreeable things to the nervous system.

I began to think about turning back. But which way, exactly, was back? I decided to go north just a little while longer, then loop back southeastward in the general direction of the road. That way, there'd be at least some possibility I could still bump into Carla Shreve, though her existence had begun to seem more and more problematic.

All I ran into in the northerly direction was one smallish, very glossy black bear, who disappeared promptly into the manzanita. I gave up around noon and started my return loop. I followed a promising ridgeline for an hour, but then it plunged over a cliff. I decided that a return loop wasn't quite the thing, and nightfall found me at the campsite of my previous night. I didn't have any more bad dreams: I was too tired.

I decided to backtrack the next morning, but when I'd climbed back up to the ridgetop from which I'd descended two days before, I had trouble remembering how I'd ascended it on my way in. I started down a familiar-looking gully, but after I'd followed it for a while, it started trending north instead of southeast as it should have. Things weren't going well. I hadn't brought that much food, and you need a lot of energy under such circumstances. You can't just totter along: you easily can fall and get hurt.

The gully began to swing *west*, and I decided to climb out and have a look around. The sides were too brushy for comfortable climbing, but a little side gully ran northward, and I followed it hoping it would lead to a spur of the ridge. I expected it to steepen and narrow quickly, but it began to get wider and leveler. Suddenly I found myself in some of the biggest Douglas firs and western hemlocks I've seen outside of Redwood National Park. Some of them must have had ten- or twelve-foot diameters.

Mountains may seem like nothing but steep slopes from a distance, but they can conceal a surprising amount of level space, remnants of the days when they were not yet mountains, but plateaus or plains. The Klamaths were like the Okefenokee Swamp forty million years ago, and there are still places in them where you can stand a mile or so from some jagged, snowy peak and imagine you're in Georgia. Little bits of the past get hoisted thousands of feet in the air as the drifting continent cracks and piles up.

I saw a patch of sunlight green through the dark trees and moved toward it over ground that got wider and wetter, the boisterous creek of the gully turning into a series of quiet pools. I pushed through a willow thicket into a sandy, grassy place. Carla Shreve sat before a tent, writing in a notebook. She looked up and saw me, crawled into the tent, and came out with a rifle, which she pointed at my nose.

"Take off your pack and step away from it," she said. "I'll shoot you if you don't. Nobody will ever know."

I did. She emptied the pack on the ground hastily: food, stove, Swiss army knife, toilet paper, maps, first aid kit, pots, pans, and so forth. She pulled the sleeping bag out of its sack and unzipped it. That she found nothing out of the ordinary didn't seem to reassure her. She had the depressed, pensive aspect of someone wavering between screams and sobs.

"I was a friend of Tom's," I said.

"I was a friend of Tom's too," she answered. Then she crawled into the tent again. I wondered what she'd come out with this time. A bazooka? But she didn't come out at all. I heard the mosquito net being zipped up. Evidently the interview was over. A great one for closed doors, this Carla. But she was crazy if she thought I was going to simply disappear now.

I could see her point about the mosquito net. It was getting toward evening, and the small reticent mosquitoes that haunt the Kalmiopsis made it unpleasant to stand still. I hastily put my pack in order, leaned it against a tree, and took a walk.

It wasn't quite the place for strolling. The ground got damper and the vegetation thicker: marshes of cobra plants and lilies, thickets of Port Orford cedar and swamp laurel. Even in open, grassy areas, the ground trembled and sank at a footstep. I pushed my way to the mossy shore of a pool that proved surprisingly deep once I saw through the glare of the water's surface. Half a dozen large, mottled salamanders rested on the bottom. They looked more green than blue at that depth, but there was no mistaking the unusual shape. They somehow seemed more comfortable than the ones in Limestone Creek.

Chapter Seventeen

I HEARD THE HISS of a backpacking stove as I walked back to Carla's camp. They sound very loud in these silent places. Carla was sitting in front of it, fiddling with aluminumware.

"Would you like some tea?" And a very merry unbirthday to you. I didn't see any dormice or hatters around, or white rabbits or talking caterpillars.

"All right."

"You must be the forest ranger. Tom always said he was going to introduce me to you."

"I used to be one."

Carla put hot water and a tea bag in a green enameled mug and handed it to me. "Sugar? Milk?"

"No, thanks."

She dabbled her tea bag, laid it carefully aside, blew the steam and mosquitoes off the top, and took a sip. I did likewise. Nothing like a tea party to establish the proprieties.

"Have a cookie," she said.

"Thanks."

She'd turned the stove off, and my teeth made a lot of noise on the brittle cookie. It was one of those Japanese rice things.

"I suppose it was because you knew his wife."

"Excuse me?"

"That he never introduced me to you."

"He never even mentioned you." There was an awkward pause. I decided to jump in with both feet. "Did you know he was dead?"

"No, I didn't."

"You didn't seem too surprised."

"I didn't? What makes you say that?"

"You didn't even ask what happened."

"What is it you want, Mr.—? I don't even know your name."

"Kilgore. George Kilgore."

"What is it you want?" Not an easy question to answer.

"I guess I want to know what happened."

"And you came here to ask me?"

"I didn't say that. You're being defensive."

"A man I've never met comes to my door telling me about a murder and then follows me into the wilderness and tells me I'm being defensive?"

"I'm not implying you had anything to do with it."

"Who said you were?"

Our voices had been rising, and the silence around us seemed very deep when the conversation paused. Carla put down her empty mug and turned to one side, tapping it impatiently with her finger.

"Don't you care about it?" I said.

She didn't answer.

"Don't you want to know what happened?"

"I don't know that I do."

"Tom's wife said you'd known him a long time."

"That's none of your business. I haven't seen Tom for a long time. I'm sorry he's dead. I'm not that surprised."

"You aren't?"

"I thought you noticed that."

"Why not?"

"Look, will you stop interrogating me? I don't know what happened to him."

"I don't know anybody else to ask about it."

"I'm sorry, but I want you to leave me alone."

"It's public land."

"All right, *I'll* leave." She stood up, then sat down. "Shit, I can't leave. But get the hell out of my campsite."

"Are you going to shoot me if I don't?" I immediately regretted saying that and crept away. I loitered awhile and finally made a camp on the other side of the willow thicket.

I cooked some food, and as I was finishing eating it, Carla appeared, looking impatient but resigned.

"If I tell you what I know, will you leave?"

"Actually, I don't really know how to get back to the road from here."

She looked even more impatient. "What do you want to ask me?"

"A lot of things."

"*What* things?"

"How about why you threatened to kill me when I came in here?"

"That's obvious, isn't it? I was afraid of you."

"Why?"

"What would you be if a stranger came around talking about murders?"

"Why do you keep a rifle?"

"Bears."

"You have trouble with bears?"

"I've had trouble with bears." End of that subject.

"Why did that woman in the post office come to warn you?"

"She's a friend."

"Does she do it every time somebody comes looking for you?"

"You may not believe this, but it hasn't happened before."

"Are you afraid somebody's going to steal some of your rare salamanders?"

"Is somebody?"

"Huh?"

"What do you know about them?"

I told her about Limestone Canyon. She'd been standing, but

now she sat down against a tree and looked at the sky, which was turning dark blue. A robin was singing in the thickets. I waited for her to say something, but she didn't.

"You discovered these creatures here?"

She didn't answer for a while, then looked at me. "Yes."

"Must have been a thrill."

"It was more than that. It was—." She shrugged. "I knew there was something in here. The U.S.G.S. has it wrong on the contour map. This is supposed to be a narrow gully."

"No kidding."

"I don't know how they made such a mistake. The aerial photos show an extra dark blotch of forest here, too broad for a gully. These little swamps are time capsules. They're leftover bits of the Miocene. The dragons live here the same way they did fifteen million years ago."

"Dragons?"

"They're related to species in China that are called dragons. The hynobiids. They're the most primitive living salamanders. These are the only members of that group in the Western Hemisphere. They're a unique relict."

"Impressive."

"It is."

"Enough to make Tom Blackwell jealous?"

She gave me an angry look, then shrugged again. "He had to have so much. It wasn't enough just to learn. He had to have a position; he had to have a reputation; he had to have a wife to take care of him."

"A lot of people want those things."

"I didn't say he wanted them. I said he had to have them. I don't think he really wanted them that much."

"I don't follow you."

"It's the difference between desire and compulsion."

"He was compulsive? Aren't we all?" She didn't answer. "You mean he was off the track? Wacko?"

"Why do you have to speak in such a flippant, trite way?"

125

"Oh, I don't know."

"Tom was like a Chinese box, you know, the kind you keep opening and there's always another one inside?"

"That's a pretty trite image."

"Is it?" She stood up.

"Hey, wait, I'm sorry I said that."

She already was walking out of the camp. She passed through the willow thicket without cracking a twig. The robin had stopped singing. It was very quiet.

Chapter Eighteen

I PASSED A SLOW NIGHT, not having a tent. I wondered if the mosquitoes biting me were the same kind that had shared Miocene swamps with Carla's dragons. What did they bite then, ground sloths? I suppose one dominant mammal is as good as another to a mosquito. Eventually they either stopped biting or I went to sleep anyway.

I woke with the sun in my eyes. Lying in a down bag in full summer sunlight with three days' worth of dried sweat, insect bites, muscle aches, and sunburn is not a supreme joy of the outdoors, especially after a largely sleepless night. I thought for a minute I'd have to unstick my eyelids with my fingers, but they finally obeyed my facial muscles. It was midmorning. Carla's camp seemed deserted. I had some tea and oatmeal and felt better, then thought of washing off some of the grime and maybe shaving.

I found a path leading from Carla's camp and followed it around a big thicket of blossoming azaleas to a pond that was more accessible than the others because of some boulders beside it. Carla was sitting on one of these, naked, combing her hair. Her body was tanned a darker gold than her eyes. It occurred to me that the sun glitters on pubic hair in much the same way as it does on pine needles.

"The water's cold, but it's clean," she said. A fallen log extended to the middle of the pond, a valuable wilderness amenity. Every pond and lake needs a nice, warm, smooth, fallen log so that you don't have to wade out through the ooze and so that you can get out of the icy water quickly after your dip.

It had been a while since I'd been invited to a secluded swim by a naked woman, and it showed when I took off my pants. I wasn't too dismayed. Genital tumescence seems to have evolved as much for display as for insemination (which could be accomplished much more simply), and it's nice to fulfill one's evolutionary functions, in proper company, of course.

"You're a healthy physical specimen," said Carla and went on combing her hair. I walked to the end of the log and lowered myself into the water, which quenched my internal fires as effectively as any other Victorian remedy.

"Ahhh! God!"

"It's a steady fifty degrees all year," said Carla. "There must be caves under here. These springs are very active. They just boil up in places."

"Too bad they aren't hot springs."

"You'd think they might be with all this volcanic rock. But there's not much geothermal activity around here. Fortunately."

My submerged legs looked pale blue and gigantic, a water sprite's legs. I saw a movement at the bottom.

"Your dragons are in here."

"They're in all the pools."

"Aren't you afraid we'll pollute the water?"

"We're not made of petroleum."

"Seems strange to go swimming with an endangered species."

"I've been doing it a couple of years, and they don't seem to mind. They aren't on the endangered list anyway."

"They won't be until you tell people about them. How's their reproduction rate, anyway? Is the population stable?"

"Read my book."

"You wrote a book about them?"

"I'm writing one."

"Will people be interested in a book about rare salamanders?"

128

"They'll be interested in one about a pretty woman exploring the wilderness."

"Oh-ho. I thought you didn't care about recognition?"

"I care about recognition when I've earned it."

The water was too cold. I supposed Carla stayed in it for hours, studying her dragons. I flailed around, trying to warm up, but moving made the water seem even colder. I crawled onto the log and tried not to shiver too conspicuously. A nasty purple-eyed elk fly started dive-bombing me.

"When you've earned it? You think Tom stole some of your dragons, tried to rip you off?"

"Maybe he found some somewhere else."

"You don't believe that?"

"No."

"Did you tell him about them?"

"Yes."

"Then he must have stolen them. Unless you gave him some."

"Why would I do that?"

"I don't know."

"I don't see the point of this speculation."

"He doesn't seem to have been very upfront with you."

"So I killed him?"

"I didn't say that." Carla was already on her way back to her camp, wearing a pair of flip-flops. She was a healthy physical specimen too. I dunked myself in the pool again. I tried pretending I was a salamander, but it was still too cold, so I climbed back on the log and tried pretending I was a turtle. The elk fly wouldn't leave me in peace, so I shaved, soaplessly and scratchily, and got dressed.

The rest of the day wasn't very productive, although I did manage to wash some socks and underwear in the creek below the dragon pools. Carla ignored me, apparently very busy taking notes on something herpetological. I didn't know what to make of her. She didn't seem like a dragon lady, despite the gun and the secretiveness. There was something almost tediously upright about her, almost prim and proper. But there was also a certain

129

craziness under that, and under the craziness I thought I sensed some kind of basic decency. I could have been mistaken. Chinese boxes. I climbed up on the ridge and did some birding, trying to keep my mind off golden thighs. I got good looks at a green-tailed towhee and a Townsend's solitaire. That was something.

By late afternoon I'd admitted to myself that I'd made a mess of approaching the woman. I went down to her camp and found her still scribbling in a notebook. I asked her to dinner.

"I'm a vegetarian." I restrained myself from saying that I might have known she was and persevered.

"I've got vegetables."

"I'm pretty busy."

"Look, I'm sorry I barged in on you. Why can't we be friends? I won't interrogate you anymore."

"In that case."

Not asking questions of a recent acquaintance is easier said than done, but I had the cooking to keep me out of trouble. I mixed the freeze-drieds with some spaghetti, olive oil, and oregano and somehow got the proportions right so that it wasn't oily or dry. I'd picked some berries during the afternoon, so we had a nice dessert.

"Thank you, George; I'd forgotten how tired I was of cooking for myself."

"You need a wife to take care of you." She let that pass.

"You were friends with Tom for a long time?"

"Since elementary school."

"He told me about some of your escapades."

"Fond memories of boyhood."

"What did *you* think of him?"

"Actually, now that you mention it, I think he was like one of those Chinese boxes. For somebody who talked so much, he seemed to have an awful lot of secret compartments. I don't know if I ever saw to the center."

"Do you think people have centers?"

"I don't know. I suppose so. I don't know if there's much in them. Maybe paper clips and rubber bands, what you usually find in a secret drawer."

"Tom seemed so full of good things when I met him. He was like Santa Claus's sack to a little biology junior. It didn't even matter if he was married. There seemed to be enough for everybody."

"Things seem like that when you're in college."

"He made everything so interesting."

"Himself especially."

"Yes, but that was okay. He was connected to everything. He had so much energy."

"So what happened?"

"What do *you* think happened?"

"What happens to everybody sooner or later. He ran low on energy. Ran into obstacles. Started looking for shortcuts."

"I don't think that happens to everybody."

"Well, it happened to me, so I understand it. Maybe he fell in with the wrong crowd. You were in Central America with him. What happened there?"

"What do you mean?"

"You went on collecting trips with him there."

"Who told you that?"

"His ex-wife."

"Well, it wasn't quite like that. We traveled together some. I was on my own trips."

"Tom told me he was smuggling cocaine."

"I wouldn't know about that."

"Did you know he was using it?"

"You said you weren't going to interrogate me."

"It's hard not to when you start being evasive."

"It's hard not to be evasive when you start being pushy."

"What's so pushy about asking one little question?"

"I wasn't interested in Tom's drug experiments. I didn't like some of the people he knew."

"What kind of people?"

131

"I don't know. There were some commercial collectors. Poachers and smugglers."

"Did you ever meet a guy named Alec Rice, a rich guy?"

"No."

"Could some of those people have been dope traders too? What did they look like? Any Guatemalans?"

"Goodnight, George." She faded into the willows again, leaving me with the campfire I'd built to provide the right confiding atmosphere. I still couldn't tell whether she was hiding things or genuinely above that sort of thing. At least she was calling me by my first name.

Chapter Nineteen

I HOPEFULLY HEADED for Carla's swimming pool the next morning, but she wasn't there. She hadn't been in her camp either. I took a dip anyway, good for me (it didn't seem *quite* as cold), and hung around idly until lunchtime. At least she hadn't broken camp and sneaked away. I was grateful for that.

She reappeared as I was gnawing on a piece of rye crisp. She had a way of fading in and out of that willow thicket that was a little spooky.

"Sorry to interrupt your lunch."

"Oh, no, that's okay. Want some?"

"No, thank you. You know, George, you might be able to give me some help."

"Sure, let George do it."

She laughed at the way I said this, which surprised me a little. She hadn't laughed before. I didn't know whether to be pleased or nervous.

"Have you done much diving?"

"Diving?"

"Scuba diving. Snorkeling."

"Can't say I have."

"How about spelunking?"

"Crawling around in caves?"

"No?"

"No."

"Are you kind of claustrophobic?"

"Not that I know of."

"George, I've been studying the dragons for two years now, and I still haven't been able to observe them breeding. I've watched them at night and at every season, but I haven't seen mating or eggs."

"Oh."

"I've decided there must be caves under these pools that they breed in."

"Sounds logical."

"The trouble is, I haven't been able to see the entrances to any caves in the pools."

"Hm."

"I'm thinking that the cave entrances are hidden by mud and debris."

"So you want me to dig out the bottoms of the pools to see if there are any entrances to the caves that you think might be there?"

"One pool, George. And not just you; I'll dig too. I've been afraid to do it by myself. I tried a couple of times, but it just didn't work with one person."

"Hard to see why not when it's a simple thing like digging a hole in the slime eight feet down in fifty-degree water."

"You don't have to."

"No, I'll help. You wouldn't happen to have a spare wet suit or Aqua-Lung around?"

"Well, no, but I have face masks and garden hose."

"Garden hose?"

"To breathe through."

"Ah."

"I've taken all the dragons out of the pool. One of us can dive down and fill buckets with the debris while the other pulls up the rope and dumps them."

"You've got buckets?"

"Actually, they're plastic jugs with the tops cut off. They're very good for scooping up mud."

"But they float."

"I can sink them down to you with rocks."

"I float too. Are you going to weight me down with rocks?" I saw myself anchored to the bottom ooze while plastic buckets weighted with big rocks dropped on my head. If she was a murderess, she was an imaginative one.

"Oh, come on, George. Use your ingenuity."

We dumped a log to the bottom of the pool (not the deepest one, but not the shallowest either) and wedged ourselves against it as we frantically scooped mud. The hose proved redundant since we got numb from the cold just about as fast as we used up the air in our lungs. We took turns scooping and standing at the surface to draw up the mud. We had quite a respectable mud pile when we gave up in late afternoon. We didn't have a cave entrance.

We didn't really *not* have a cave entrance. We simply never got much of anywhere. We didn't even hit anything hard except the odd tree branch or old bone, green with algae. It was like trying to excavate a Thik-shake, except Thik-shakes taste better.

"Agh!" said Carla as I rose from my twentieth immersion in the methane-rich gray and green stuff. "You're like the creature from the black lagoon, George!"

"That right?" I assumed a lumbering monster gait and chased her around the pool a couple of times. Since we weren't wearing anything, this would have been erotic if she hadn't been as covered with slime as I, and if she hadn't begun to be visibly upset after the second circuit. I got back in the water like a good monster, and she called a halt to the digging not long afterward and went off to get dressed. I went to wash myself in the creek and discovered that ooze is hard to get out of the hair. I was still trying to get it all out fifteen minutes later when Carla came into my camp to ask *me* to dinner. It seemed the least she could do.

"Boy, you're really *interested* in these dragons, aren't you?" I said after we'd consumed a not-too-distinguished bulgur wheat concoction. I could see why Carla liked a respite from her own cooking, although maybe she was just having a bad night.

"Yes, I am."

"Why do you think that is? I used to wonder about Tom. I can understand people being interested in whales or birds, but I don't know about all these little, creepy things. I mean, the dragons are a nice color, but they don't *do* much."

"They do what we do. Eat, breed, die."

"Yeah, but you know what I mean."

"I've been watching them for two years, and I haven't seen everything they do. Nothing is boring if you pay attention. It's boring people who get bored."

"Thanks."

"Don't be paranoid."

"I'm not."

"Yes, you are. You're one of the more paranoid people I've met. I bet you're in the dope business."

"Let's talk about salamanders."

"They interest you?"

"They're beginning to."

"Well, there's a lot of folklore about them. Tom was interested in that. He always said they were animals of power. He liked Castaneda's books."

"You mean rising out of the fire and all that?"

"You're well read for a forest ranger."

"I'm not a forest ranger anymore."

"For a dope businessman, then."

"I'm in reforestation, actually. Silviculture."

"Why don't we climb up on the ridge and watch the sunset?" It was a way to escape the mosquitoes, so I went along with the diversion. Carla was not to be rushed when it came to divulging information. When we got to the ridgetop, the sun was just on the horizon, striking scarlet sparks on conifer needles.

"The soil here is volcanic," said Carla. "That's why the trees around the swamp are so big. It's very fertile."

136

"Not like peridotite."

"The peridotite is like a fortress around these trees. They would have been cut years ago if it wasn't for the peridotite all around them. The trees would have been cut and the dragons might have been exterminated before science discovered them."

"Tell me more about this salamander folklore."

"You seem to know about it already."

"Just that they rose out of the fire. Witches and alchemists used them."

"Actually, it was the phoenix that rose *out* of the fire. The power of salamanders was that they could live *in* fire, even extinguish it with the coldness of their bodies and the poisons in the skin. It's a different symbolism than the phoenix. Not renewal, endurance."

"Must have been a comfort when people were dying of fevers and being burned at the stake."

"They burned salamanders and used the ashes as medicine. The skin secretions may have medicinal properties. One of the relatives of this species is still used that way. It's called the white dragon, and it lives in a lake on a Chinese mountaintop. The Chinese dry it and use it for stomach remedies."

"Tom might have thought your dragons have medicinal properties?"

"The idea interested him. People are always saying some obscure endangered species is going to produce a substance that will cure cancer. There's magic in the idea that some hidden power in nature could save lives. People wouldn't revere science the way they do if it didn't have power to save or transform life, if it was just a neutral model of nature. I think Tom wanted to have some power over life with his science, but it was hard. It's the physicists and chemists who have the power, not the biologists."

"What about recombinant DNA and genetic engineering?" I said.

"That's biophysics and biochemistry. Tom wanted a power alive *in* nature, not just in a laboratory. Not a legend or myth that you'd need imagination to understand. A real, physical power, but natural, not artificial. He wanted people to have faith in living nature again, not just in artifice. Fire's a fundamental artifice, isn't it? We're consuming the world with artifice, burning the forests, even the fossil forests."

"Little fish that stop big dams have power."

"But the snail darter didn't stop the Tellico Dam. That's the trouble with all this power seeking. If you killed a white dragon, it was supposed to cause a deadly storm, but that didn't stop people from killing them for stomach remedies. If my dragons could cure cancer, they'd be trampled in the rush," she said.

"What about if they could stop the dam in Limestone Canyon?"

"They didn't, though, did they?"

"Would you have given Tom some if you thought they would?"

"Why do you keep coming back to this?"

"It's an interesting ethical question."

"You're interested in ethics?"

"Sure I am. What do you mean by that?"

"Mean by what?"

"You think I'm some kind of criminal?"

"Who said anything like that?"

"What makes you so noble?" I said.

"What are you talking about?"

"Nothing."

"It sounds like you have a guilty conscience."

"At least I admit it."

"You do? I haven't heard you admit anything."

I obviously wasn't going to have the last word, so I started climbing back down the ridge. It was much darker when I got back under the trees. There was nothing to do but go to bed. I slept better than I had before. Either the mosquitoes were tired of me or I was getting used to them.

Chapter Twenty

THE POOL WE'D TRIED to excavate had settled and cleared by the next morning, but no cave entrance was visible, just the same old oozy bottom, maybe a foot or two deeper now. I made a pole from a dead sapling and probed the bottom with it. The pole was about twenty feet long, and there was at least one place on the bottom that would swallow its whole length, but Carla made me stop because she'd put the dragons back in and didn't want them disturbed anymore.

Carla spent the day sifting through the ooze we'd dumped beside the pool. She found cartridge cases, broken whiskey bottles, some bits of steel that might have been parts of leghold traps, and a miscellany of antlers and bones, including the largest leg bone I've seen outside a museum.

"What is *that*?"

"Probably from a bear. I'm not too up on mammalogy," said Carla.

"Awfully big bear."

"Might be from a grizzly. Things last a long time in this cold ooze."

"Seems kind of long even for a grizzly."

"Some of the Pacific Coast grizzlies were exceptionally large. Think it's a Bigfoot bone?"

"Hm. What are you looking for?"

"Dragon bones, of course. To grind up for magic potions."

"Didn't the Chinese use dragon bones for aphrodisiacs? Are you going to slip some in my soup?"

"Those weren't salamander bones. They were fossils of prehistoric mammals, including early hominids. Salamanders don't really have much in the way of bones, and they're so small and delicate that they don't last very long. I haven't found much."

"And you say they've been here for fifteen million years?"

"I'd *love* to find some fossils. That's another reason salamanders get neglected. There's so little evidence of their evolution that scientists have nothing to theorize about, nothing to write controversial papers on."

"If you found some fossils, it would put you ahead, eh?"

"Always looking to the highest motivations, George."

The smell of the ooze hadn't improved much, and I was afraid Carla would put me to work again, so I took a walk. I spent a while on the ridge with my map, seeing if I could identify landmarks that might guide me back to my pickup. Some peaks to the north probably were the Chetko Rim, a semicircle of mountains that contains the Chetko River's drainage. I couldn't make much of anything out of the ridges and knolls that rambled off in other directions. I could see logging roads and clear-cuts in the hazy distance, but no trace of a trail.

I climbed halfheartedly up and down a few ridges. My appetite for exploring the Kalmiopsis was glutted for the moment. I was beginning to get nervous about my seedlings and my property in general. There didn't seem to be much more I could learn from Carla, not that I'd learned much. I had a feeling she was honest, if not confiding, and that she really didn't know about cocaine smuggling. It takes a certain effort to get into the low life; you can skate over all kinds of unpleasantness if you don't stop to look down. That was my predominant feeling anyway. I had subordinate feelings that she might be mainlining heroin in her tent or plotting to blow out my brains while I slept. I supposed I was a little paranoid.

I didn't have much reason for hanging around: time to return

140

to trailer and seedlings and ailing garden. I found the thought a little depressing. When I got back to my empty camp, I found it even more depressing. I peeked through the willows and saw Carla bent over her notebook. I could have invited her to dinner again, but I was running low on food, and it seemed a little pointless.

As I said, when you have feelings in the wilderness, you have them big. I sluggishly ate some ill-cooked rice and greasy-tasting sardines and then lay back, stunned with gloom. Empty sky, dull trees, whining mosquitoes, stinking socks. Even the robin sounded mindless and aggravating. My metabolism felt at such a low ebb that I could almost see the sun move as it sank toward the ridgetop. I was glad when it set: mindless, aggravating sun. I lumbered off to wash my dishes in the creek, didn't do a very good job, lumbered back, and got into my sleeping bag. I wished I'd brought a book, something violent, pornographic. At least I didn't have trouble falling asleep.

I awoke with a start, heart pounding. I'd heard a noise in my sleep. This is not unusual in wilderness, where various creatures come to investigate your campsite. It is unusual to look around after such an awakening and see an eerie red light filtering through the trees. It was coming from the swamp.

It's a little hard to get an undershirt on over a head of hair that is standing up, but I did (backwards, I later realized). I blundered into the rest of my clothes, picked up my flashlight, and lurched toward the swamp. When I got close enough to the red glow to see what was on the ground, I narrowly missed stepping on one of the dragons. It crawled sedately away, ignoring me. I ignored it for a few steps, until I realized that it was the first time I'd seen one out of the water by its own volition. I did a double take, scratched my head, and stumbled toward the red light again. I found it hanging from a cedar, a red lantern, with Carla sitting motionless under it, looking at two motionless dragons.

"Why are they leaving the water?" I asked.

"To feed."

"What do they eat?"

"Look for yourself."

"Some teacher you'd make."

"There's too much teaching, not enough looking."

"How can they just come out on land after living under-water?"

"You should know that. They're amphibians. They get oxygen through the skin, the mouth membranes, and the lungs. This species also retains vestigial gills in adult form, which is one of the unique things about it. It's the only neotenic species that leaves the water. Partially neotenic, anyway."

"Neotenic?"

"Immature salamanders have gills. Some species may breed when they still have gills. Then they're called neotenic."

"Why do they do that?"

"Good question. Some salamanders become neotenic if a trace element is lacking from the water they live in. I don't know about these, though. They haven't responded to any chemicals I've tried."

"I don't see any gills."

"Good, you're starting to look." Carla picked one up and showed me little slits behind its head. "The gills are shrunken and internal instead of bushy and external like the larvae's. They open these when they're underwater." The dragon de-cided it didn't like being held. It blinked, and made walking-away movements. "That's another unique trait. Other neotenic species lack eyelids."

"Like fish."

"The dragons fertilize their eggs externally, like most fish. At least the ones in China do: I don't know about these. That's why the group is considered primitive. Most salamanders fertilize their eggs internally." Carla put the creature down, and it moved away six inches and stopped, as though that was far enough.

"Hm. Frogs fertilize their eggs externally, don't they? That means they're more primitive than salamanders?"

"God, you're like a little kid." She took the lantern from the tree and started toward her camp. "I'm chilly. Want to have a campfire?"

"Hey, yeah! I have a little rum. We can have hot toddies. That is, if you drink alcohol."

"I drink." Things were looking up. I dashed around collecting downed wood and had a crackling blaze before she could change her mind. I mixed the toddies big and strong. Scheming bachelor.

"Agh, George. What proof is this stuff?"

"Just ordinary Puerto Rican rum."

"I guess I'm not used to it. Anyway," she continued after a few lengthy sips, "the most primitive frog in these mountains fertilizes its eggs internally. The male has an extension of his cloaca that looks like a little pink penis."

"How shocking. So frogs started out by fertilizing their eggs internally?"

"Not necessarily. These frogs evolved internal fertilization because they live in fast creeks. The sperm would be swept away in the current if the male didn't use his little organ. They call him the tailed frog. To be truthful, they should call him the penised frog. That sounds a little awkward, though. Maybe the pricked frog."

"Goodness."

"The cocked frog? The dicked frog?"

"Awfully vulgar."

"Accurate."

"So did salamanders start fertilizing internally because they lived in fast creeks?"

"Why do you keep asking all these questions, George?"

"I'm curious by nature. And I find you interesting."

"I find you interesting too." An embarrassed pause. "When you're not being annoying."

"I aim to please."

The conversation drifted into silence. We finished the toddies, and the fire died down. An owl was calling somewhere. Carla's face was in darkness when she spoke again.

143

"Did the mosquitoes give you a hard time last night?"

"Same as the other nights."

"You could sleep in the tent if you like."

"I wouldn't want to put you out."

"It's a two-man tent."

I crashed through the willow thicket and got my sleeping bag, almost dashing my brains out against an overhanging tree limb. Carla had disappeared when I got back, evidently into the tent. I sat at the entrance and wrestled myself out of my clothes, crawled in, laid out my bag, got into it, lay there for a long silent moment, then reached over and touched warm skin in the darkness.

"I get so horny all alone in this place," said Carla.

Chapter Twenty-one

CARLA WASN'T IN THE TENT when I woke up. She wasn't at the swimming pool either. I hung around awhile, then went to my camp and made breakfast. When I heard movements across the willow thicket, I went over there again, stifling a desire to ask where she'd been. She had taken down the tent and was putting it in a stuffsack.

"Morning."

"Good morning."

'You're leaving?"

"I've got to get back and do some writing."

"Can I come?"

She didn't answer.

"I might go off with some dragons if you don't keep an eye on me."

"I'm not sure I like the way you think, George."

"It was a joke, for crying out loud."

"Was it?"

"You liked the way I thought last night."

"That's crude."

"Hah!"

"You got me liquored up."

"Oh, come on."

145

She kept on packing, but a little less stiffly. "Last night was nice, George, but I've got an awful lot of things to do."

"So do I. I have to go back and take care of my seedlings."

"Seedlings?"

"Pine and fir seedlings."

"Well, hurry up and pack."

"Yessum."

Carla's way out was in the opposite direction from the way I'd come in, but that didn't surprise me. She marched along confidently although I saw no sign of a trail or blazes.

"You really know this route, huh?"

"I've walked it enough."

"Tom come here with you?"

"Yes."

"When was that?"

"A long time ago." Ever-confiding Carla. It wasn't the best situation for confidences, hiking offtrail in the Kalmiopsis. Carla followed ridgetops for the most part, but there were some exhausting bushwhacks and climbs up and down canyon walls.

The farther we got from the dragon swamp, the more doubts I began to have about the impressions I'd formed there. Carla marching ahead of me seemed shadier than Carla sorting through the swamp ooze. I thought of all the questions I could have asked her but hadn't. Of course, she probably wouldn't have answered them. Why had I been so tolerant of her evasions?

What could I do, though? I could tell Grunewald, but somehow I didn't think he'd be that interested; and if he was, he wouldn't be pleased that I'd waited so long to tell him about Carla. Carla wouldn't like it if I set the police on her anyway. I'd have them both mad at me.

We got to the road before sunset. My route going in had been pretty loopy. Carla loaded her Land-Rover in a no-nonsense way, moving boxes around busily, then got in the driver's seat. I walked over and leaned against her window to stop her from zooming away immediately.

146

"Dr. Todd at the Bayview Museum told me to say hello," I said.

"Give him my regards."

"I'm afraid I told him about the dragons in Limestone Creek."

"Afraid?"

"I thought you didn't want people knowing about them."

"Just the wrong people."

"Wrong people?" Carla didn't answer. "What wrong people do you mean? Somebody who wants to steal your dragons?"

"No. I just don't want people nosing around." Uncomfortable silence.

"When's your book coming out?"

"George, I've got to do some shopping."

"Can I call you sometime?"

"I don't have a phone."

"I'll drop you a line."

"All right."

"Come and visit me next time you're in California." I gave her my phone number. "Want to know what I find out about Tom?"

"Oh, I don't know, George. I don't know." She wheeled away in a cloud of dust. She'd parked her Rover in the return direction, so she didn't even have to turn around.

I spent another night driving, just me and my radio, whenever I could get something on it. I was heading eastward from Eureka when I tuned in a late news broadcast.

"The body of an unidentified man was found in the Klamath River below Weitchpec yesterday. Sheriff's deputies said the man is believed to be of Indian ancestry, although the features were severely mutilated by what appeared to be a shotgun blast to the face. The body had been in the river for several days and may have floated from some point farther upstream."

I twiddled the dial a lot after that but heard not another word about a floating corpse. The media are everywhere until you actually want to *know* something. Then I got over the coastal summit into the Trinity River gorge, and the mountains shut out most of the broadcasting. The gorge is scenic in the daytime, but

147

a little spectral at night. There's fast traffic between Eureka and Redding, and every time one of the fast ones would come up behind me to pass, I'd wonder if it was a two-seater, red pickup.

It might not have been Jimmy, of course. Weitchpec is in Hoopa Valley, the biggest Indian reservation in California. If the radio had said that the body pulled from the river was that of a Guatemalan named Jimmy, I'd have run to the sheriff. But what if it wasn't?

"You see, sheriff, I'm working for this large-scale dope smuggler and mass murderer over by Hayfork, and I think he might have shotgunned this Guatemalan revolutionary agent who works for him too. Why don't you go up there, take a look around?"

It was still dark when I reached home. I wished I'd taken longer to get there. I thought of taking the back drive in, but it seemed pointless. If somebody was waiting for me, they'd see my lights coming on the back drive as easily as on the front. So I pulled in the front fast and nearly ran over Lewis, who sat blinking in the headlights. No two-seater pickup. I left the truck lights on and prowled around for a while, but everything seemed all right. I went inside, turned on all the lights, and had a drink. Lewis went through his ritual in a perfunctory way, then climbed into my lap. I think he was relieved to see me. I had another drink.

I turned on the radio, but there was still nothing about a floating body. I felt like waiting for the morning news on television, but I was too tired. Aside from that, I didn't feel too bad, considering that I was in fear for my life. It must be good for the glands.

I felt worse when the telephone woke me in midmorning. My head ached. It was Grunewald.

"You're back at last," he said. "I was about to put out a warrant for you."

"I?"

"Just kidding. I think we know who killed your friend. There's going to be an arraignment tomorrow, and I want you to be there."

"Tomorrow?"

"You want to see justice done? Come to my office around noon."

"Who is it?"

"Be here tomorrow and you'll find out. I may want you to testify."

"Anybody I know?"

"Could be. I've got another call. See you tomorrow."

I'd never heard him in such a good mood. He hadn't even asked me where I'd been.

Chapter Twenty-two

I GOT TO GRUNEWALD'S OFFICE early and had to sit in the corridor for twenty minutes while he had a vituperative conversation with a well-coifed man in a three-piece suit who popped out of his door without a glance at me. Grunewald followed, looking a little haggard.

"You eaten yet?" he asked. "Come and have a sandwich. The hearing starts at one." We went around the corner to an unappetizing-looking diner. "Don't order anything hot. The pastrami on rye isn't bad. How was the drive?" I told him. He wasn't listening.

"Does the name Angel Rivera ring a bell?"

"Angel Rivera?"

"I didn't think so. He hasn't been here long."

"Been here?"

"He's an illegal alien. Colombian. Sometimes you do get lucky."

"He killed Tom Blackwell?"

"We got a fingerprint. An *undocumented* fingerprint. That was a treat. One time in a hundred you find a fingerprint, a *nice* fingerprint, on a glass ashtray, and nothing. Two hundred million sets on record, and they can't make it. We have to pay for that little service now; takes a lot of computer time."

"They couldn't make an identification?"

"Nope. But I had a bright idea. Only in America do we import criminals. Did you read about the big coke smuggling bust week before last?"

"No."

"Yeah, why should you? Might get on your nerves. Anyway, we had a pile of illegals in the net, so I looked at the fingerprints before they started slipping overboard."

"And you found him?"

"No. But I kept looking, every time an illegal came through the door. Bingo. Not only that; we got a weapon. This guy is going to be here longer than he thought. Land of opportunity."

"What was he arrested for first?"

"One of the coke bust people fingered him. Personal grudge."

"So he's involved in cocaine too?"

"Is an Arab involved in oil?"

"Why did he do it?"

"What, kill your friend? He owes us an explanation? He's got an attorney. He doesn't even speak English. Maybe your friend stepped on his socks. We don't worry about motives that much anymore. People don't seem to *have* motives that much anymore."

The rye bread was on the woody side, and the pastrami was anointed with cheap yellow mustard, but the macaroni salad and garlic pickle weren't bad. Everything dropped into my stomach with almost-audible clangs. Grunewald didn't finish his.

"What'll they do to him?"

"That's not my department," said Grunewald in a German accent. "Feed him for many years to come. Not that I envy his diet." He looked at his plate. "Not that I weep for him either. They'll cut a deal. He'll be out in a few years if he's good. Though from what I've seen of this one, he won't be good. I'd put my money on a violent end."

"In prison?"

"It won't be at the Top of the Mark."

151

The hearing was over almost before it started. Grunewald and a well-dressed man waved papers around; another well-dressed man waved more papers around; both well-dressed men exchanged arcane legalities with the bench; and the prisoner, a slight man with green eyes and curly beige hair, was led away, appearing as uncomprehending as I.

"Well, that's it," said Grunewald. "We got an indictment."

"You don't need me to testify?"

"What, you disappointed? Don't be. You wouldn't like it."

"Can I ask you something?"

"What? I got a meeting."

"Did you think I might have done it?"

"I thought you might have."

"What made you think I hadn't?"

"Catching Rivera."

"That's all?"

"You want a character reference? Murderers don't usually report their crimes."

"I almost didn't report it."

"Aren't you glad you did? Call me sometime. I'll give you the latest on our friend downstairs."

Grunewald left me with the same baffled, unfinished feeling as he had the last time he'd summoned me south. I didn't feel like driving back straightaway, but I didn't feel like a night on the town either. I fed my meter and wandered over toward the Bayview Museum again. It's a nice museum, even if you can't see the bay from it. I suppose you could before the Oakland downtown redevelopment. There was a new exhibit in the lobby: photographs of Central Valley native grasslands and marshes, very colorful, with spring green willows and rushes and purple and gold vernal wildflower pools. It didn't look like the valley I'd driven through in the morning.

The volunteer receptionist was less casual than before. She made me sit down while she got Dr. Todd on the intercom. He curtly told her to send me in. When I got to his door, I could see through the little wire-reinforced window beside it that he had another visitor. The visitor turned around when I opened the door. It was Alec Rice.

"Hello, George," said Dr. Todd. "George Kilgore, this is Phil Murray."

Chapter Twenty-three

ALEC OFFERED ME his hand without a flicker of recognition. I shook it. Maybe he *was* somebody else. A sense of unreality surged over me, as though I'd just taken a strong hit off the top of the plant. My heart raced, my mouth dried up, my palms sweated. I sat down in the chair Todd offered (after first removing a pile of California Native Plant Society bulletins) and tried to act normal.

"Phil has given us some very excellent invertebrate specimens from the Sonoran Desert. It's really a help because we can't afford to send anyone now, and we're trying to fill our new exhibits."

"Are you a biologist?" I asked.

"No, I'm a layman." It was Alec's voice. That made me feel a little saner for some reason.

"For a layman," said Dr. Todd, "he certainly knows how to find some fascinating things." He pointed to a small terrarium on his desk, which contained what looked like the biggest centipede I'd ever seen. It had long orange horns on the front and back ends.

"I just use a little basic ecology," said Alec modestly. Not quite in character.

"Was there something you wanted to talk about, George?"

"I was at the courthouse, and I thought I'd stop by. They caught the guy who killed Tom."

"I heard. A vagrant, was it?"

"An illegal alien."

"Did they find out why?"

"Why he was killed? I guess not. Something to do with drugs." Todd shook his head. There wasn't much to say. I suddenly wanted to go home. I stood up.

"Sorry to interrupt your meeting. I've got a long drive." Alec looked at his watch.

"Actually, I've got to run along too." I ended up walking down the gray corridor with him. There was more activity today: people were sitting at desks, talking on telephones. Tom's half office was still bare, though. Staff reduction through attrition, with a vengeance.

When we got to the lobby with the nature photographs, Alec stopped and turned his most charming smile on me, as though we'd just shared a clever joke. I didn't smile back, though I felt a certain urge to. Then he looked serious.

"Tom Blackwell was a damned good naturalist. Too good for what was happening to him here."

"What?"

"He had an eye on him that you don't often find with these academic types. Good hands too."

"Hands?"

"Some people have a gift for that. Tom could handle anything without hurting it and without it hurting him. I've seen him pick up rattlesnakes as though they were kittens."

"When did you see this?"

"Tom and I are old associates."

"Tom and *you*? Who the hell *are* you?"

"I guess we should talk about that. Why don't you come over to my place for a drink?"

"Your place?"

"I've got a place in San Francisco. I'll show you my collection."

"Collection?"

"I'm an amateur naturalist, like the man said." He started walking out of the building, and I followed, zombie-fashion.

"I don't understand, man. Why didn't you tell me any of this?"

"They hadn't found Tom's killer."

"So?" Alec looked at me and raised his eyebrows.

"What, you thought *I* might have killed him? How did you even know I found him?"

"I told you. We were longtime associates. I take care of my people. Tom had told me about you. We were thinking of getting you involved. I'm serious about the reforestation."

"Involved in what? This is bizarre. What's your real name, anyway?"

"Come on over and talk about it if you want. I don't like standing around the street." He sounded mildly interested in the prospect of my visit. Alec was a good salesman. He made bored little movements as I stood speechless. I wanted to ask about Jimmy, but it didn't seem like a good idea. I wanted to go home, but I was just too *interested* in the ball of yarn he was handing me. I accepted with a sinking sensation. He wanted me to go in his car, but I insisted on following him in the pickup.

Alec drove a diesel Mercedes. I followed it across the Bay Bridge to a nondescript little warehouse south of Market. He opened a big steel door and ushered me into a long corridor with new hardwood floors and white plaster walls. Ferns, bromeliads, and orchids hung from the ceiling; and, instead of pictures, recessed terrariums and aquariums decorated the walls. They weren't just little boxes with a few mosses or tropical fish, but steamy, watery spaces as big as Pollocks or de Koonings, with big, colorful creatures in them: a school of what might have been golden trout, a dozen kinds of turtles, a tropical swamp with iguanas and boa constrictors.

"More interesting than paintings, don't you think?"

"More expensive to maintain too." I was trying not to seem impressed.

"And more interesting to maintain. We've had some breeding successes that might surprise the big zoos and aquariums if they knew."

"Why don't they?"

"Trade secrets. If they knew, they wouldn't need to buy from us."

"From us?"

"Tom and I were associates."

"Selling animals to zoos?"

"I did the selling. Tom did the breeding and most of the collecting."

"He was collecting animals and selling them to zoos?"

"We sold about as much to private collectors as to zoos, actually."

"You mean like rare animals? Endangered animals?"

"Oh yes. That's where the market is. You'd be surprised how many people collect."

"Tom was a conservationist. An environmentalist."

"Of course. Collecting seldom wipes out a healthy population. We pick up the pieces after the ranchers and farmers and miners have put their feet through the ecosystems. You might as well blame somebody for picking up pieces of stained glass and carving after somebody's dynamited a cathedral. That's what you're trying to do with your tree nursery, isn't it? Pick up pieces?"

"It's not the same as trading in rare animals."

"It's not? You're trying to make a living, right? Trying to breed organisms that are being decimated in the wild? Selling them on the open market? Where do you get your seeds? You like the virgin forest; we all like the virgin forest, but where would you be if it was still virgin?"

While I gnawed on this, Alec led me into a richly appointed living room and put a glass of expensive whiskey and a delicious little cigar in my hands. I could see a study with ceiling-to-floor bookcases through an open door.

"Timber's a necessity, not a luxury."

"Beauty's a necessity too. There's nothing more beautiful than healthy, living animals."

"Wait a minute. Tom told *me* he was smuggling cocaine. Not rare animals."

"Did he?"

"You didn't pay for all this selling rare animals."

"Of course not."

"Well?"

Alec shrugged. "Tom wasn't too clear about some things. He may have felt guilty or ashamed. I certainly never let him have anything to do with the business, but, of course, he knew about it."

"He told me he was smuggling cocaine because he was ashamed of what he was really doing?"

"Maybe."

"Then why was he murdered? People don't kill each other over rare species."

"Oh? No, I don't think that was why. Much less interesting than that. Just a woman."

"A woman?"

"Angel Rivera's a jealous man. They'd both been involved with the same woman. Maybe you know her, Carla Shreve?"

"No."

"I thought you were an old friend of Tom's?"

"We hadn't talked much recently."

"Have another?"

"No, I've got to get back."

"I've got a more comfortable guest room down here. Stay the night. It's a long drive."

"Got to water my garden."

"Let me show you something first." He motioned through the door at the aquariums in the hallway. "This stuff isn't much. Let me show you what we have downstairs. I'm really going to miss Tom. I don't think I'll find anybody as good as he was. Of course, he was impractical. It would have been better if he'd been some-body I could trust with the business end too."

The whiskey was working on me. I knew Alec was leading me with his little tidbits of information, but I wanted the next tidbit, and he was so articulate, so reasonable. I felt a certain fellowship: just a couple of entrepreneurs trying to make it in a self-destructing world. There was something else, something strange. I was kind of sorry for him. He seemed very alone, as though Tom Blackwell had been his last friend on earth. All these expensive toys, and nobody to play with. But then maybe he wanted me to feel sorry for him. I should have learned by this time not to trust any impression I got from Alec. Or maybe I really was just feeling sorry for myself.

I followed him through a tile-floored, copper-sheathed kitchen to another steel door. It opened on a flight of brick steps.

"Come on, it's not a dungeon."

"Who said anything about a dungeon?"

Several short flights of steps ended in a tight, concrete space with another steel door. Alec unlocked it, and we entered one of the newest, shiniest laboratories I've seen. Like the hall upstairs, its walls were lined with aquariums and terrariums, but accessible from the room, not recessed. An impressive array of tubes and gadgets protruded from them, so that I thought of patients in an intensive-care unit. Alec stopped in front of one that contained a small school of not-very-impressive minnows.

"Ever see an extinct species in the flesh? Meet the Pahranagat spinedace, *Lepidomeda altivelis*, which officially departed this life in 1959."

"Shit. Where did you get them?"

"Trade secret."

"What are they worth?"

"Now who's being mercenary? They aren't worth anything. They don't exist."

"What are you going to do with them?"

"Do with them? I don't know. Maybe I'll breed a lot of them and turn some loose in suitable habitat. See what the scientists do."

"You're playing God."

"It's fun." He pointed to a terrarium that contained a number of tiny, brilliant pink and blue frogs. Several had attached themselves to the glass with their toe pads: you could see their translucent throats moving as they breathed. "This is another species scientists aren't aware exists, but in this case they've *never* known about it. It comes from one valley in the eastern Andes. Nowhere else."

"Don't you want to report it so you can get credit for discovering it?"

"What credit? A pat on the back from some Ph.D. while he jacks up his career on it?"

"What about Tom?"

"He wasn't too eager for his activities down there to be publicized."

"Are you eager?"

"You think they're going to molest me for smuggling frogs? It's the best cover in the world."

The next aquarium contained an assortment of popeyed little fish that perched on the bottom, using their pectoral fins as forelegs. I recalled them from New England brooks.

"Darters."

"I've got the Maryland, the Niagara, and the sharphead: all on the federal list."

"Not the snail?"

"Too famous. Like owning the Mona Lisa. Vulgar."

"This whole room is full of endangered species?"

"They are, they were, or they will be." He crossed to another steel door and unlocked it. I followed him into a taller room, brilliantly lit. The noise in it was deafening after the silence of the laboratory. The room was so completely soundproofed that no whisper of its cacaphony of shrieks, whistles, giggles, and caws had escaped before Alec opened the door. There were a lot of potted plants. It smelled somewhere between a hothouse and a poultry barn. The smell gripped at my throat.

There were parrots, monkeys, eagles, trogons, and dozens of

160

other creatures I barely recognized. I saw what I thought were lemurs, and some of the Hawaiian birds I vaguely remembered from my Peterson *Field Guide to Western Birds*. Alec said something I couldn't understand because of the noise. He motioned me to a cage containing two white, black, and red woodpeckers with cream-colored beaks. He smiled at my look of shock and shouted in my ear.

"I was asking if you were a birder. These aren't ivorybills, though. Not even I have those, though I may know of someone who does. These are imperial woodpeckers from Mexico. They're getting about as rare as ivorybills were here in the 1930s."

It was a relief to step back into the silent laboratory with the fish and frogs: sluggish creatures, indifferent to fate. The raucous monkeys and parrots cut closer to the bone.

"Doesn't it make you sad?"

Alec shook his head. "I'm not a sentimentalist. Everything dies. When I die, I won't miss anything. That's a fact. These creatures don't know they're endangered species. They live better here than they would in the wild. We deparasitize them and feed them regularly. They probably think they've gone to heaven."

"I thought human survival depended on the survival of other species."

"That's an environmentalist platitude that happens to be true in the long run. But then it's sentimental to worry about human survival. People want their children to succeed so they can be proud. They don't care about the human species any more than they do about the snail darter. They don't even like being human. What, meat-eating primates from Africa? They'd rather be sunbeams or computer games. Fun in this life and fun in the next, if possible. After that it's a throwaway container."

"And you're having fun?"

"Damned right. Aren't you?"

"Not all that much, I suppose."

"You're a sentimentalist. I bet you give money to those save-this and save-that scams."

"Now and then."

"You don't have the energy to get what you want. Think about it. You'll get a lot more out of life if you're not weighed down with all that negative bullshit."

There were so many kinds of fish, reptiles, amphibians, and small mammals in the laboratory that I almost hadn't noticed a small aquarium on the long table that ran down the center of the room. Turning around, ready to leave, my eyes swept over it and returned. There were two dragons in it. I looked at Alec, and he looked back.

"Where did you get those?"

"Where do you think?"

"Where do I think?"

"You're an awful copycat sometimes, George."

"From Tom?"

"Indirectly."

"What do you mean by that?"

"Tom didn't tell me about that little scheme. I don't think I would have approved. Too risky, too sentimental."

"He was trying to get some self-respect."

"To live outside the law, you must be honest."

"Hip platitudes."

"It would be fun to breed them. Do you know where I can get more?"

"No."

"I think maybe you do. My collector's heart would pay dearly for that kind of information. This is really an unusual species. Really unique."

"What's unique about it?"

"A number of things. We don't need to go into them right now."

"Cancer-curing chemicals?"

"Environmentalist platitudes, George. I want it: that makes it unique. As long as I'm alive, I'm going to get what I want.

162

That's what being alive is for. I'm willing to pay for useful information."

"Try Limestone Creek."

"Don't be disingenuous. I know Carla Shreve is captivating. I found her so myself. But I wouldn't trust her. She's like a female Don Juan, you know? Bad case of penis envy."

"I don't know what you're talking about."

"I got her address from Todd today. I'll look her up myself."

"What do you want more for?" I asked, wanting to change the subject. "You've got two."

"They're both females."

"How can you be sure?" Alec didn't answer. "They all look the same to me."

"You're beginning to irritate me."

"Maybe you should take another look at them."

"All right, George." Alec rolled up his sleeve, reached into the tank, and picked out one of the dragons. He took a little gold and ivory penknife out of his pocket and slit the dragon's belly open from jaw to tail. He held it up to me, the blood running down his wrist. "See? Female."

Alec dropped the writhing dragon into the sink and washed his hand, then started toward the door. That is, he started toward *a* door. I suddenly realized that I wasn't sure which one of the four steel doors in the room was the one we'd entered from. They were identical. But I didn't think it was the one Alec was moving toward.

I backed up against the nearest other one and tried to turn the knob. It was locked. They probably all were, from both sides. Alec took out a set of keys and turned to me.

"You ready?"

"That's not the door we came in."

"No, it opens on the street." He unlocked it and opened it a little way, but not enough for me to see anything but shadows. "I thought you wanted to go home?"

"That doesn't look like the street."

"We're down two flights. You think I'm going to throw you

163

to the crocodiles? The American crocodile is endangered, you know." He laughed. Then he looked at me with contempt. "Go on. And watch your ass, like the man said."

I stepped through the door, and he slammed it behind me. My eyes were accustomed to the brilliant light in the laboratory, and they saw nothing for a moment. Then they discerned a faint reflection of daylight above, and I stumbled up concrete steps toward it.

Chapter Twenty-four

PLAYING THE RADIO while you're driving the freeway at night is like being in touch with the spirit world, all these ragtags of humanity sifting out of the air. Just south of Willows I dialed in an eighteenth-century Border ballad—fiddle, flute, and drum and a man's and a woman's voices—that might have been broadcast from Edinburgh in 1760. It started conventionally enough as a lament over growing old, the singer complaining that hearts had beaten faster when he'd been a young man walking down the street. Then it got stranger and stranger, with the singer going on to say that the only heart that beat as he walked now was his own, that he walked in a valley where the sun never shone, and so on, until you realized that the singer was a ghost who'd been haunting a place so long that not even his bones remained there.

I knew how he felt. Driving the freeway at night is a disembodied-enough sensation, and Alec, or Phil, had done a thorough job on my reality sense. I'd never even found out which was his real name, if either of them was.

The moon was full, and the Sacramento Valley grain fields were washed-out platinum, a distinctly ectoplasmic color. Dry grass is a subtle reflector of moonlight: the shiny stems give off an almost phosphorescent glimmer. The man-made stuff—culverts, power lines, machinery—reflected the moonlight less, so

165

they seemed even more ghostly than the land, mere shadows, smudges. Even a freeway rest stop that I pulled into seemed spectral, the lights around it surrounded with so many flying insects that the whole place had a gossamer, wavering aspect. The lavatory was full of big brown moths, and of crickets that crawled under the toilets and urinals stridulating, echoing the high-pitched din that came from their brothers in the grass outside. I sat down on a bench by a eucalyptus tree and began hearing whispery little voices and midget ensembles of bells and drums in the stridulations. I needed a rest.

I felt a little better when I pulled into my driveway and saw Lewis sitting in front of the trailer. Things were normal: if they weren't, Lewis would be hiding. I was so glad to see him that I picked him up and gave him a squeeze. He jumped out of my arms and ran up to the trailer door, demanding to be let in.

I felt a little worse when I went into the barn to check on my seedlings. It smelled dry in there, not moist and humuslike the way it was supposed to. I flicked the light switch, and nothing happened. I got a flashlight from my glove compartment and looked at the seedlings. They weren't withered yet, but they were dry. I went to the fuse box and was relieved to see that one was blown. It might have been worse. I replaced the blown fuse and heard the little pump that supplies water to my overhead sprinklers go on.

When I looked again the next morning, I found a number of seedlings that probably were too stressed to grow well. It's not enough just to grow trees: they have to grow fast and straight. Clients would not be amused by groves of picturesquely gnarled bonsais. I culled the damaged seedlings and replanted the flats. It was getting a little late for that, but I thought I might get lucky.

It kept me busy for a couple of days. When I wasn't replanting, I weeded the garden, picked vegetables, and made myself time-consuming meals. After that, I watched reruns on television. One night I fell asleep in front of it, and didn't wake up until the first program came on the next morning. The confident voice of the early newscaster gave me a turn.

166

The morning after that, as I was putting on my pants, there was a knock at the door. I peeked out of the bedroom, but I couldn't see who was behind the screen.

"Who is it?"

"Trinity County sheriff's department." I waited for further explanation, but there was none. I went to the door, shirtless and shoeless, and opened it. There were two deputies on the porch. I knew one of them.

"Well hello, Marvin." Marvin Healey had worked under me as a seasonal forestry aide a couple of summers. He'd been one of those very serious, conscientious underlings who like to ask questions about why you want a certain thing done a certain way and who sometimes have better ideas about how it might be done. I've found that the best way to handle such underlings is to make fun of them in an easygoing, friendly sort of way. It hadn't endeared me to Marvin.

"Mr. Kilgore?"

"That's the name." Marvin had done a good job of picking up the official sheriff's deputy's tone of voice.

"We wonder if you could come to headquarters with us for a short time this morning and lend us some assistance?"

"What kind of assistance?"

"I'm not at liberty to divulge that information now, sir. If you'll come with us, I'm sure it will be explained."

"I think I'd rather you explained it now." They didn't say anything. I'd been holding the door open. I started to close it, but Marvin Healey's foot was in the way. "Hey, Marv, will you get your foot out of my door?"

"Pardon me?"

"I said get your jackboot out of my door, you fucking storm trooper." I reached through the opening and pushed him in the chest.

The next thing I knew, I had my face in the driveway, handcuffs on my wrists, and Marvin's knee in the small of my back. They picked me up and slung me into their back seat, then sat in front for an excessively long time, writing on their clipboards or

167

listening to their radio. I was about to say something witty when they suddenly sped away, throwing me off the uncomfortable balance I'd achieved. Riding in the back seat on an uneven gravel drive with your hands cuffed behind your back is not one of your basic skills, even at moderate speeds. I could hear the gravel their tires had thrown up hitting the trailer behind us. I finally righted myself after we'd been on the blacktop of 299 for a while, but I still tended to flop over on the curves.

Pretty soon we were driving through suburban Weaverville, and I sank down in the seat voluntarily. People would find out about this anyway—in small towns there are people who know more about you than you know about yourself—but I preferred not to be there when they did. I didn't do too badly: the only spectators when Marvin and his friend pulled up at headquarters and hustled me inside were two children of a couple with whom I had a nodding acquaintance.

They sat me on a bench in the corridor for about five minutes. I got some interested looks. Then they took me into a small bare office. Grunewald was sitting at the desk. The deputies plunked me into a chair, took the cuffs off, and marched out.

"No shirt, no shoes, no service," said Grunewald.

Chapter Twenty-five

"YOU GOING TO READ me my rights?"

Grunewald picked a pencil from the desk and began fiddling with it. "What rights? I'm not arresting you."

"What *are* you doing?"

"Of course, I could if I wanted. Abusing and assaulting an officer."

"What are you doing here?"

"Will you just for a goddamned minute stop asking questions? Always asking questions."

"Under the circumstances—."

"Shut up! It's your turn to answer questions. How did you find out about Blackwell's girlfriend?"

"His girlfriend?"

"Kilgore."

"Through his ex-wife."

"And how did you find his ex-wife?"

"Through directory information."

"Damn, I'm going to kill Murphy."

"Huh?"

"Nothing. Why didn't you tell *me* about the girlfriend?"

"You didn't ask. I mean, I thought you probably knew."

"How about telling me about her?" I told him about Carla.

He leaned back and closed his eyes. "She said she hadn't seen him in months?"

"Something like that."

"She was lying."

"What makes you say that?"

Grunewald rubbed his hair. It was thinning on top. "I'll answer that," he said. "Your friend's nextdoor neighbor came back from Europe two days ago and said he saw a woman coming out of Blackwell's apartment just as he was leaving for his trip. He left for his trip the day before Blackwell was killed."

"Oh."

"We've had some more interesting discoveries. Rivera's attorney pointed out that the ashtray in Blackwell's apartment was the same kind they have in the rooms at Rivera's hotel. The ashtray was heavily used, but Blackwell didn't smoke, right?"

"Not tobacco."

"All of a sudden I'm railroading helpless immigrants. People are getting nervous."

"Wasn't there a gun?"

"He didn't buy it or register it or even leave a print on it. We found it in his drawer, next to the Gideon Bible."

"He was set up."

Grunewald was silent, strangling with impatience. I told him about Alec's connection to Blackwell.

"You're a real mine of information. Got anything else for me?"

"I thought you'd caught the killer."

Grunewald shifted in his seat and rubbed his hair again and stood up. "Come on," he said. "We're going to go talk to your lady friend."

"What's she got to do with it? It's a day's drive."

"She's a potential witness, that's what."

"Why don't you talk to Alec Rice?"

"Because he wasn't seen leaving the apartment. Look, Kilgore, you want to stay here?"

"Here? No."

"Well, you're not leaving without me, and I'm going to Cave

Junction. I've got a witness's statement that a woman was seen leaving that apartment, and it's my job to interview that woman, and I'm going to do my job and get paid and pay my taxes so you can sit up here and get food stamps."

"I don't get food stamps."

"You're going to need them if I don't get some cooperation." He walked out of the room and was gone about fifteen minutes. He seemed in a better mood when he returned. "They're sad to see you go. They say to be sure and let them know if you misbehave."

"Do you mind if I get a few more clothes?"

"No, I want to take a look at your place anyway."

"Got a warrant?"

"Just a friendly visit."

"If we're so friendly, why didn't you just come yourself, instead of sending the Cossacks?"

"You worked for the government, Kilgore. Protocol."

"She may be in the wilderness, you know. We may have to hike in."

"I brought my sneakers. We can have a safari."

Grunewald was driving an unmarked vehicle, so I was spared notoriety as we got into it and drove away. Half-naked hippies are still a fairly familiar sight, even in 1984. I didn't escape completely, though: John Minarik was standing in front of the trailer when we drove up. Lewis was sitting beside him, as though they'd been chatting about my shortcomings.

"Are you all right, George?" he said, politely averting his eyes from my bare torso. "I saw a sheriff's department vehicle up here. Thought there might be some trouble."

"Hi, John. No problem. This is—Mr. Grunewald. John Minarik, my nextdoor neighbor."

Grunewald smiled and nodded.

"Lucky you."

"Excuse me?"

"It's a good thing you dropped by, John. I'm taking another little trip. Maybe you could keep an eye on the place again."

"Going away for long?"

"Just a few days."

"You've been getting around the past few weeks."

"He's a rover, all right," said Grunewald. "Let's go look at your tree nursery, George." Minarik went off, shaking his head, and after putting on a shirt and shoes, I led Grunewald to the barn.

"I'll be damned; they really are trees. You plant every one of these little things yourself?"

"Every one."

"Looks like a lotta work. Why don't you just grow dope like the rest of the guys?"

"I like trees better."

"An idealist."

"A neurotic. Too much anxiety."

I threw my backpack, sleeping bag, and some food in Grunewald's trunk, and we set off, at a speed consistently higher than posted limits, though I didn't bother pointing this out to Grunewald. I couldn't resist cowering in my seat as he roared past some of the larger trucks. It seemed to amuse him. Highway 299 has a lot of blind curves and steep shoulders. It's pretty breathtaking in spots along the Trinity gorge, although it doesn't jump out at you. At first you just see a mass of dried-out-looking Douglas fir, but then you get glimpses of rock walls dropping hundreds of feet to a river like a string of emeralds. Sometimes you drive along level with the vultures that patrol the gorge.

Grunewald took a look down one of the drops and shook his head. "Godforsaken country."

"I thought you came fishing here when you were a kid?"

"Yeah. Give me Yosemite or the Grand Canyon; you can have this place. There's something screwy about it: always gave me the creeps."

"Too many spirits."

"Too many weirdos talking about spirits."

The gorge is so deep that it comes as a surprise to see how far it is above sea level once you've passed through Willow Creek and started descending the hairpins leading down to Eureka.

The Pacific shines so brightly that you can't see any horizon line, as though the land is bordered with some kind of silver ether instead of ocean and sky.

Grunewald had no comment on the Pacific. I had time to think about matters of concern—what Carla had been doing at Blackwell's, if she had been there; what Alec had to do with it all—but I just felt drowsy. Grunewald woke me by stopping for gas in Eureka. We had lunch in a drive-in, then drove north through the redwoods, astonishingly lush after the desiccation inland.

"How about redwoods? You like redwoods?"

"Sure, I like redwoods," Grunewald replied.

"Seen one, seen them all?"

"My patio is redwood."

"I bet it looks like all the other patios."

"I built it myself. It's a nice patio. Doesn't mean I don't like these guys." He gestured at the three-hundred-foot-tall guys looming over U.S. 101. "I'm a Democrat. You grow redwoods in your barn?"

"I'm too far inland."

"You should grow redwoods. Put your money where your mouth is."

"There's too much money where my mouth is right now."

It was dark when we got to Carla's house. The Land-Rover was in the shed, and a faint light was coming through the roadside window. Grunewald drove many yards past the house before he parked. He took a pistol out of the glove compartment, and a big patrolman's flashlight.

"I don't want any monkeyshines, Kilgore. Just do what I say, all right?"

"You won't need a gun with her."

"Yeah, and what about that rifle?"

"She was scared."

"They're all scared. That's why they kill people. Just go up and knock on the door."

"What are you going to do?"

"Let me worry about that."

Chapter Twenty-six

G RUNEWALD STOOD beside Carla's door while I knocked on it. There was no response. He motioned me to knock harder, and I did. We heard a window open, and Carla's voice asking who it was.

"George Kilgore."

"George? What is it?"

"Uh. We need to talk." Grunewald and I craned our necks, but we couldn't see the window she was talking from. Evidently it was screened by live-oak foliage. We didn't know if she could see us.

"I was in bed, George."

"Sorry."

"Wait a minute."

The window closed, and there was a lengthy silence. Then footsteps approached the door, and it opened. Carla hadn't gotten her gun, but she had gotten dressed. She was lit faintly by a light farther inside: there wasn't any light on the porch. She looked at me, then turned her head as Grunewald stirred beside me.

"I'd like to ask you a few questions, Miss Shreve."

"Thanks a lot, George."

"You shouldn't have been so secretive."

"I have a right to privacy."

"Nobody's going to violate your privacy," said Grunewald.

"What if I don't want to answer your questions?"

"Come on, Carla, you were seen coming out of Tom's apartment the day before he was killed."

"No, I wasn't."

"You answer the description, Miss Shreve." Carla put her hand toward the door as though to start closing it, then checked herself. She turned around and disappeared back into the house. Grunewald and I followed her into the living room, where she had dropped down on the sofa.

"Why don't you make us some coffee?" said Grunewald.

"Screw you, buddy."

"Not you, him. Brother, you feminists."

"Screw you," Carla repeated.

"Make us some coffee, okay, Kilgore?"

I went into the kitchen and made some coffee. It was a nice kitchen, clean and neat. I wondered how she kept it that way. My kitchen sweats dust and grease and grime. I made too much noise finding things to hear much of the conversation.

They were silent when I came in, a frustrated silence. They picked up their coffee cups with relief, but after a couple of sips, I could see them starting to feel aggressive again.

"It's my professional responsibility," said Carla, as though this were the last word on something.

"Yeah, well, it's *my* responsibility to get all the evidence."

"It isn't evidence."

"You're not the one to decide that."

"It's not my decision. I promised Tom I wouldn't divulge it."

"Promises to the dead aren't binding."

"What isn't evidence?" I said. They both looked at me disgustedly.

"Blackwell wrote and asked Carla to come and see him. Said it was important for his professional career. She drove all the way to Oakland, and he gave her something and made her promise not to show it to anybody."

"Kind of a dumb thing to do."

175

"What, trust me?"

"No, just dump something on you like that. What did he seem like?" Carla grimaced. She was beginning to get the same unhappy look she'd had after holding me up with her rifle in the dragon swamp.

"Stoned, probably. Distant. Abrupt. It—hurt me to see him. I didn't stay long. I was angry. But he asked me not to tell anybody about it, so I haven't."

"You've told us now," said Grunewald. Carla didn't answer. "It must have something to do with the murder."

"Herpetological data? What would that have to do with a murder?"

"It might have a lot to do with it." Grunewald told Carla what I'd told him about Grunewald and Alec Rice, a.k.a. Phil Murray.

"Murray? Tom was *working* for him?"

"You knew Murray?" Carla looked the way many women do when they hear about snakes or salamanders.

"I didn't want to know him."

"He spoke well of you."

"What's that mean?"

"He implied that you'd slept with him and with a Colombian named Angel Rivera. He told me Angel Rivera killed Tom because he was jealous over you."

"I never heard of Angel Rivera."

"So what *about* your herpetological data?"

"I just don't see what four pieces of paper could have to do with all this."

"What kind of paper?"

"I promised Tom."

"A promise to a cokehead and a smuggler?"

Carla started to cry. Grunewald and I blinked at each other. Carla got up and disappeared through a door that led farther into the house. We waited a moment, then followed her down a flight of stairs to a room with a large picture window looking out on the starlit hills. There were bookshelves, a dissecting ta-

176

ble, aquariums. Everything looked second- or thirdhand, but it was clean and neat like the kitchen. The aquariums were empty.

Carla opened a filing cabinet and took out a manila folder, which she handed to Grunewald. I looked over his shoulder as he opened it. There were four photocopies of topo maps, slightly dim and ragged photocopies. They looked like parts of U.S.G.S. quadrangle maps, though the quadrangle names weren't on them. Most of the place names were Spanish, so the maps probably were from the Southwest. Somebody had drawn a dotted line in red ink around a small area in each map.

I began to get anxiety symptoms again: speeded heartbeat, sweaty palms, dry mouth. No wonder Alec wanted to find Carla. I was surprised he hadn't arrived already.

"So what the hell is this supposed to mean?" said Grunewald.

"I told you, he didn't explain it to me."

"What do you *think* it means?"

"They look like collecting sites."

"Collecting sites?"

"There might be rare species there. Maybe Tom didn't want Murray to find them."

"He was protecting these rare species against poachers? He was a poacher himself. Why would he do that?"

"Maybe he was trying to get some self-respect."

"Those aren't collecting sites," I said.

"Oh yeah? What are they, Deppity Dawg?"

"Gravesites."

Chapter Twenty-seven

I TOLD THEM about Jimmy. Grunewald shook his head.
"I could have been an insurance investigator, you know? If
people withhold information, they don't get their claims paid off.
A nice, sensible job."

"Well, how was I supposed to know it was related to this?
Jimmy told me he'd never heard of Blackwell. I had other things
on my mind this morning."

"They were talking about that corpse in the river at the sheriff's office this morning. The dental work wasn't American, and
there were no fingerprints on record."

"How was I supposed to know?"

"You never talked to the sheriff's department at all, did you,
Kilgore? You're really something, both of you." He grabbed
Blackwell's maps out of Carla's hands and slapped the top of the
filing cabinet with them. "Solid citizens."

"There's a credibility gap."

"Yeah, you're incredible."

"Well, you've got a motive now."

"Tell me about it."

"Alec, or Phil, or whoever he is, killed Tom because he had
evidence of the murdered refugees."

"And what was your friend doing with this evidence?"

"I don't know."

"And why did he give it to Carla here?"

"I don't know. So Alec couldn't get it."

"Pretty tenuous."

"All you have to do is go to the places on the maps and dig."

"Yeah, I'll do it on my next vacation." Grunewald was starting to seem impressed for the first time since I'd met him. "There were rumors last year—how many people did he say this guy had killed?"

"Several hundred."

"Where's your phone?"

"There isn't one," said Carla.

"That's right. I need some sleep anyway. We'll worry about it in the morning."

"Alec said he was coming up here."

"I know, Kilgore. That's one thing you did tell me."

"Yeah, but I thought he was looking for salamanders."

"Now you know how it feels to be a salamander."

"You really want to spend the night out here?"

"Maybe he's already outside, waiting."

"Hey, come on, Grunewald. You don't know this guy. He's scary."

"All the more reason to stay here. Always keep a tight perimeter at night, that's what we learned in 'Nam. We didn't learn anything else, but we learned that."

"You're not taking this seriously."

"Yes, I am."

To prove his seriousness, Grunewald made me sit at the front window for the next two hours while he and Carla slept. It was a long time to sit in a dark room looking at a dark road, and I dozed off a couple of times, but never for very long. Every time the house creaked or the wind rattled the metal roof, I'd wake up with my scalp crawling. I had Carla's rifle, but it didn't seem like much. I kept thinking of the automatic weapon fire lighting up the woods around Alec's ranch. I heard a creak in the corridor, and my scalp crawled again, even though I knew it was Grunewald coming to replace me. He looked tired.

179

"See anything?"

"No."

"Doze off much?"

"Not enough so I wouldn't hear a pickup coming."

"Yeah? Sleep's a funny thing."

"I don't think anybody came."

"Hope not."

"You think you can stay awake?"

"Hope so."

I went into the living room and lay down on the couch. Carla was asleep in a bedroom off the kitchen: I could hear light snores. Women always sleep better than I do. She hadn't said much after showing us the maps. I would have liked to talk to her, but I couldn't think of anything to say.

I felt thirsty and went to the kitchen for a drink of water. The tap whined when I turned it on, and I heard Carla stir, but she didn't say anything. I went down to the study and looked out the picture window. There was a dark ravine of oak and pine and a bare rocky slope above that. I had to get close to the glass and crane my neck to see much sky. The Milky Way looked more like a plume of gray smoke than a drift of stars. I suppose it looked so palpable because there was no moon. It looked low enough to touch the treetops. The close-packed stars didn't throw any light into the trees as the moon would have. I couldn't see anything under the treetops.

I went back to the couch and lay listening for a long time. Something landed on the roof with a faint scampering sound. An owl or a flying squirrel, I hoped. I wondered if I should get up to see, but I was beginning to drift. Then the room was gray with dawn.

I looked out the window and thought it must be pretty early still because the sky was gray, but then I realized that it was overcast. I looked at the clock in the kitchen. It was already seven. I went into the front room and found Grunewald asleep in the chair by the window, his head back and his mouth open. He looked vulnerable, a little soft, like any middle-aged, white-

180

collar worker with a redwood patio in Orinda or Hayward. He stirred, as though disturbed by my presence, and opened his eyes. He closed his mouth with a snap, then opened it again.

"Shit. What time is it?"

"Seven."

"Shit. I'm getting too old for this."

"We're still alive."

"Any coffee?"

"I'll make some."

"How about some bacon or something. I'm hungry."

"Carla's a vegetarian."

"Figures."

"There might be eggs."

We went into the kitchen and found Carla putting water on to boil.

"See any murderers?"

We didn't answer that. I helped Carla make some cheese omelettes while Grunewald went from window to window with a pair of binoculars.

"I don't see anything," he said as we sat down to eat. Carla was better at omelettes than she was at bulgur wheat.

"How could he know I have the maps," she said, "and if he knew, why didn't he come before?"

"Good question," said Grunewald.

"Yeah, well, he told me he was coming."

"You believe what this guy tells you?"

"If it's scary, I do."

"You're kind of an imaginative guy, aren't you, Kilgore?"

"Cowardly, you mean?"

"Paranoid, he means," said Carla. Things did seem safer in the morning light. Maybe Carla's maps *were* collecting sites.

"I still want to look into this," said Grunewald. "I want you to come back to the city with me, talk to the feds."

"I don't want to go all the way to San Francisco," said Carla predictably.

"You want to be subpoenaed? Withholding evidence?"

"You're like a broken record sometimes, Grunewald."

"Dealing with you two would crack anybody's disk."

"Why can't we just go to Medford or something?"

"All right, look, we'll go to Cave Junction, and I'll make some phone calls. Then we can all make up our tiny minds."

"No tricks."

"I might do a backflip or two. Stand on my head."

We cleaned up the dishes, and Grunewald convinced Carla to give him the maps and to pack a bag, "just in case." Then she insisted that she wouldn't go unless it was in her Land-Rover. Grunewald didn't like this but finally gave in. He took another look around with the binoculars, then we huddled together at the door.

"You go with her, Kilgore."

"I'm driving," said Carla.

"All right, all right. Can George take your rifle?"

"Okay."

"I'll meet you in Cave Junction. Just get in and drive away. Don't stop. Okay? Let's go."

Carla and I ran toward the shed. I saw Grunewald out of the corner of my eye, hurrying up the road toward his car. Then we were in the shed. We jumped in the Land-Rover, and Carla put her key in the ignition and turned it. Nothing happened.

There was a shot, the deep, two-syllable "ka-pow" of a high-caliber rifle. I started to open the Land-Rover door, turning to raise Carla's rifle at the same time. Carla cried out. I glanced back at her involuntarily, the door was wrenched open from outside, and Alec was there, as though he'd risen from the ground, pointing a machine pistol in my face.

Chapter Twenty-eight

G RUNEWALD WAS LYING on his side halfway to his car. His face was dusty and scraped from the fall but still peaceful-looking, as though he'd stretched out for a nap in the middle of the road. Carla started to cry, and I leaned against a tree and felt dizzy. I heard Alec shouting in Spanish and was vaguely aware of Rodrigo passing me with a long-range rifle in his hand. He grabbed Grunewald's feet and started dragging him behind a clump of manzanita. I could see where Rodrigo's bullet had hit him in the right shoulder and torn out the left side of his chest. A perfect shot.

Alec started going through Grunewald's pockets, then looked back at the road, where papers were fluttering in the morning breeze. He walked out to where the manila folder and four maps had been scattered by the impact of the shot and picked them up unhurriedly, then strolled back toward us, pausing to kick dust over Grunewald's blood.

"Is this all of it?" We didn't answer. "Let's not waste time."

"So you can shoot us quicker?"

"I'm not going to shoot you if I don't have to." I'm ashamed to say that this remark made me feel better, not a lot better, but a little better. Alec shouted again at Rodrigo, who started walking toward Grunewald's car after extracting car keys from his pocket. Then he motioned Carla and me toward the house.

183

Alec nodded approvingly at Carla's downstairs study after herding us into it. "A nice work space. A little tacky, but functional."

"Go to hell, Murray."

"Always independent and outspoken, Carla." He started going through her files. "You've got a lot of data here. Take a while to sift through it. Maybe I should just have Rodrigo burn it all."

"No!"

"Is this all of it?" He waved the folder.

"Yes."

Alec put the folder and maps in Carla's wood stove and set a match to them. "God, you're such a third-rate villain, Murray. A third-rate villain and a fifth-rate naturalist."

"You're jealous."

"Jealous of what? Anybody can buy rare species from hungry Indians."

"Spiteful too."

"You're a thief, Murray. You're not even a brave thief. You steal from people who don't know what they have."

Alec was beginning to color. I changed the subject. "How did you find this place?"

"I'm good at finding things."

"No, you're not. You're good at buying things. Or stealing them."

"You didn't mind taking my advice in Costa Rica."

"Your advice in Costa Rica was worth shit, Murray."

"You're a liar, Carla. You never would have found that god-damned plethodontid if you hadn't listened to me."

"I never would have found it if I *had* listened to you. George here knows more tropical ecology than you do. You're not even a knowledgeable thief. Just a rich one."

Alec sat on the edge of the desk. He seemed calm, but his knuckles were white where they gripped the wood.

"Since you mention it, Carla, there might be some things I'd

184

like to buy from you." He motioned toward the empty aquariums. "I thought you might have some specimens on hand."

"Specimens of what?"

"Your unique discovery. What are you asking?"

"Go to hell."

"It's a buyer's market, Carla. I'll name a price. How about a dozen specimens for George's life here?"

"Go to hell."

"Hear that, George? All right, I'll come down a little. I'll take only nine."

"This is insane."

"No, killing to get what you want isn't insane. It solves many problems."

I'd heard enough of this conversation. "*I'll* take you to the goddamned salamanders," I said.

"Don't be stupid, George. He'll kill us when we get there."

"Better then than now."

"You're a fool, George."

Alec looked pleased. "All right," he said, "let's go."

When we got outside, Grunewald's car had disappeared, and the red, two-seater pickup was pulled up next to the body. Rodrigo was standing over it with a big, zip-up plastic bag.

"Give him a hand with that, George."

"What?"

"Go on."

I helped Rodrigo zip Grunewald into the bag and then load him onto the back of the truck. I wondered if I'd dig my own grave if Alec told me to. Alec had made Carla get her backpack from the house, and Rodrigo had already gotten mine from Grunewald's trunk and loaded it on the pickup. Alec was a planner. He produced a topo map of the area and asked me to point out the site of the dragon swamp.

"I can't find it on a topo," I said, truthfully enough. "I just learned the way by following Carla."

"Are you sure you know it?"

"Yes."

Alec looked suspiciously at me, then at Carla, who ignored him. He rolled the map up and snapped a rubber band on it. It sounded like a bone breaking. He motioned Carla and me into the back seat of the truck while he and Rodrigo threw an old blanket over Grunewald.

When Rodrigo got into the driver's seat, he turned around a moment and looked at Carla. Just a look, no expression. Alec caught his eye and made an impatient gesture. Rodrigo turned back, shoved the truck into gear, and roared away so fast I almost bit my tongue. Rodrigo was showing off.

I found Carla's parking spot without much trouble. Ridgetops tend to look alike as you drive mile after mile, but this one was especially narrow. After he parked the pickup, Rodrigo went around and pulled a folding stretcher out of the back.

"What's that for?"

"You don't think I'm going to bury him right alongside the road, do you?"

"Carry a body in a stretcher over this terrain? You can't do it."

"I'm not going to. You and Rodrigo are."

"With a backpack too? You're nuts."

"You asked for it, George," said Carla.

"How am I supposed to lead the way while I'm carrying a goddamned stretcher?"

"Walk in front."

My arms were already tired when we reached the bottom of the gully separating the road from the next ridgeline. Since I was first, I bore all the weight going downhill. It was a bad day for carrying a load. The sky was still overcast, but it was warm and humid, an unusual combination for the West Coast, where clouds usually mean cool weather. Sweat didn't evaporate; it clung to my cheeks and burned in my eyes. Earlier, the overcast had looked like the kind of coastal high fog we have in the summer fairly often, a smooth, sooty pall over the heavens, but now it was clotting up into queer udder shapes. It reminded me of the overcasts they get back east just before a tornado. I wondered if

186

there was some kind of freak typhoon coming up from the Sea of Cortez.

It was still midmorning, but there were no bird calls. It was getting late in the breeding season but not that late. When I thought about it, I couldn't remember hearing any crickets the night before, although it had been a pretty warm night and I'd been awake through most of it. Of course, I'd had other things to think about.

"I don't like this sky," said Alec. "When will we get there?" He didn't sound too uncomfortable. He wasn't even carrying a backpack, having divided his effects among Rodrigo, Carla, and me. All Alec was carrying was a little day pack for his camera and binoculars and a holster for his machine pistol.

"We'd get there tonight if I wasn't weighed down. Can't say otherwise."

"We can camp out." Alec said this with a kind of joviality that for some reason scared me more than anything he'd said before. I was almost glad I had the stretcher to carry. It gave me something to pour adrenaline into, instead of running screaming into the bushes.

I toiled up the ridge, glad that Rodrigo was bearing the weight now and listening hopefully for sounds of strain. He was steady as a rock: there might have been a mule harnessed to the back of the stretcher. He probably could keep this up all day. I knew I couldn't. My knees felt shaky, and my hands were already chafing from the stretcher handles. Grunewald was getting stiff and was increasingly inclined to slide off the stretcher if it was tilted too much.

Fortunately Carla's route was mostly along ridgetops, and carrying the stretcher was almost bearable on the level. The ridgetop I started to follow seemed like Carla's route, anyway. It's almost impossible to remember a route through broken country after having traversed it once in the opposite direction. I hadn't agreed to take Alec to the swamp out of any strong intention of getting him there. I'd just wanted to end that disagreeable conversation and give myself time to think.

187

Now I had time, but I wasn't thinking very well. My brain was clotted with the garbage that rises to the surface when you're feeling exhausted and scared, snatches of radio and TV nonsense, idle obscenities. I felt as though my life had turned into one of those nightmares where you go around a room opening doors and finding the same unpleasantness behind each one. Alec seemed to have all the exits blocked.

The ridgeline I'd been following dropped away into a canyon. It didn't look familiar. The boggy smell of the alder-bordered creek at its bottom reminded me of trout fishing in New England when I was a kid. I hadn't thought about that in years. I'd used worms: not very sporting, but effective. You just let the current carry the worm downstream, and pretty soon you reeled in a trout.

I chose a gentle, open slope to climb out of the canyon, but, as slopes will, it got steeper and bushier. It became one of the jungles of young tan oak and chinquapin that cover old burns in the Kalmiopsis. The tan oak was flowering, and the cloying reek of its pollen, not to mention the hundreds of small white moths attracted to it, made breathing hard. Even Rodrigo was starting to pant. He literally had to shove the stretcher upward through the thickets.

"Ugh," said Alec, spitting out a moth. "You'd better not be lost, George."

"There's no trail. I told you it would take longer carrying this thing."

"All right, we'll bury him when we get to the top of the ridge."

The thought of digging a grave wasn't very agreeable, but I was too relieved at the prospect of resting to worry much.

Chapter Twenty-nine

A LEC DIDN'T GIVE ME any time to rest, and digging a grave in the Kalmiopsis is just about as hard as carrying a corpse across it. All we had to dig with were some little folding spades. The ground was made up of large stones packed in hard red clay once we'd dug through the few inches of leaf mold at the surface.

"Why don't you give us a hand?" I said to Alec. The silence was getting ominous. Carla hadn't said a word since we started walking and was looking very pale.

"It's what I pay you for."

"Pay me?"

"Aren't you on the payroll now?"

I didn't know what to say to that. I dragged another rock out of the clay and flung it aside.

Carla looked up at the sound. "Well, George?"

"George is a realist at heart," said Alec.

Carla looked at him. He sat against a tree, eating a chocolate bar.

"Why did you kill all those people?" she said.

"What people?"

"It must have been for money. Was Tom trying to blackmail you?"

"Tom didn't know what he was trying to do. That was his problem."

Rodrigo said something and Alec laughed. Rodrigo picked up a large rock and flung it backward over his head as though it was a feather pillow. It made a lot of noise rolling down the brushy slope.

"What did he say?"

"He said the rocks are heavy."

"That's not what he said," said Carla.

We dug on in silence. No cicadas, no wind in the trees. A yellow haze on the horizon made me wonder if there was a fire somewhere. The overcast wasn't moving. It stretched overhead like a dingy plaster ceiling, the kind they try to make look fancy with swirly textures. We hadn't even seen a bird, much less heard one, except a solitary raven in the distance. Ravens don't care about the weather.

"Isn't this deep enough?"

"A little deeper," said Alec. We hit a large tree root. "Oh, well, that's all right."

We picked up Grunewald in his bag and tried to drop him into the hole, but he didn't fit. He'd stiffened with his arms and legs splayed, and the hole was too narrow. We tried shifting him around, and he fell in a little way but then got stuck at a tilt. We had to pull him out again. I started to laugh, and I laughed for a long time, until my face was wet with saliva and tears.

"Pull yourself together, George," said Alec.

Carla was sitting with her head on her knees and her arms folded in front of her face. Rodrigo had jumped into the hole and widened it while I was laughing. He tipped the body in and began scraping dirt and rocks after it as I sat against a tree and played with a handful of pine needles.

"You should eat something," said Alec. He handed me a piece of chocolate. I put it in my mouth and chewed, but I couldn't swallow it. Finally I got a water bottle and managed to wash it down. Rodrigo finished filling the grave, stamped it down, and negligently kicked some leaves and twigs over it. Alec spoke to him, and he shrugged and raked more debris over the grave, so that it was indistinguishable from the rest of the ridgetop. Then he folded the stretcher into a small package and put it in his pack.

Alec had been studying his topo map, and he stuck it under my nose again, pointing to a small circle he'd drawn.

"I figure we're right about here now."

"Could be."

"Where's our destination in relation to this?"

"I don't know. It's not on the map."

"What?"

"Carla says the U.S.G.S made a mistake when they made this map. They made it a narrow gully when it's really a wide, level place."

"Why didn't you tell me that?"

"You didn't ask."

He wasn't listening. "All right, point to a landmark in the right direction."

I knew better than to refuse that request, even though I didn't recognize any landmarks. I pointed to a patch of thick forest on a gray stone ridge to the west.

"Is that it?"

"It's in that direction."

"You'd better not be screwing around with me, George."

"You don't have to believe me."

"You're right, I don't. Well, let's get going. Shit, Carla, you look terrible. Here, eat some of this."

"I'm not hungry."

"You should eat. Can't have any sick backpackers on our hands." Again the joviality, like a scoutmaster from hell. I was beginning to hate Alec. I hadn't really hated him before, when he was being evil, but I was beginning to now, when he also was being mean. Before, he'd seemed too powerful and smart to hate. Our emotions just aren't up to civilization. We're equipped to deal with dominant primates, not mass murderers. When we call people like Alec and Rodrigo "animals," it's a kind of wishful thinking.

The direction I'd pointed out led down the other side of the ridge into another canyon, or, rather, gully. Its lower slopes were festooned with big, mossy boulders, and it took some twisting and turning to get through them. On the other side was more tan oak and chinquapin scrub. Climbing out of a gully off-trail is hard enough under ordinary circumstances. You keep thinking you see the top of the ridge ahead, where sky shows through the trees, and it keeps turning out to be just a glade or a subsidiary knoll, with an even steeper slope above it than the one you just climbed.

Finally we reached a fairly open bench that ran along the side of the ridge. The slope above it was an impenetrable scrub of manzanita and rhododendron, so I started following the bench northward. It might have been the remains of an old mining road, though it was grown up with big pines and firs.

"You changing direction, George?"

"We have to go around this brush."

"Seems pretty random."

We were moving through a place where tall rhododendrons grew on both sides of the bench: me first, Carla second, then Alec and Rodrigo. There was a sound like a tiny jet passing overhead, and a Cooper's hawk chased a flicker past our heads. Carla dropped her pack and dived into the bushes. Before I could react, Rodrigo was after her, and Alec had the machine pistol pointed at me.

"She may be dumb, but she's feisty," he said. We heard receding crashes in the foliage, then silence. After about five minutes, Alec began to look peevish. He shouted, waited a minute, then shouted again. Pretty soon Rodrigo came in sight, pushing Carla ahead of him.

Chapter Thirty

I THOUGHT ALEC would have things to say about Carla's escape attempt, but he just told her to pick up her pack, and we started off again. At least it had put some color back in her face.

The level bench soon deteriorated into a gravelly slope overgrown with canyon live oaks. The afternoon was getting very hot despite the overcast, a brassy heat, bitter on the tongue. The fine dust from the crumbling gravel coated the pores and made the sweat on my face thick and itchy, as though someone was pouring bowls of hot Cream of Wheat over my head. When we finally reached the ridgetop, I was ready for a breeze, but there wasn't one.

"All right," said Alec, "let's make some time now. Hurry up." He gave me a little push from behind, and I stifled an urge to hit him. I walked a little faster, but he pushed me again. I turned around, clenching my teeth.

"I'm being easy on you, George. You know that, don't you?"

I turned around and walked faster. I didn't want to think about what Alec would consider being hard on us.

The ridgeline began trending west, and we didn't have to cross any more canyons for a while. It would have been a nice walk under other circumstances. The ridgetop was wooded enough to be shady, but not so much as to be gloomy. The pine duff was easy on the feet, and the only obstacles were clumps of pinemat manzanita and red and blue penstemon here and there. We walked a long time in silence. It began to get hypnotic; it seemed that things would be all right as long as I kept walking. I even began to get drowsy.

I realized that I was looking at the sun for the first time that day. It was still partly obscured by the overcast but was discernible as a bright yellow smear streaked with violet. It was in front of us, pretty close to the western horizon. I hadn't realized it was getting so late. Burying Grunewald had taken a long time.

The sun drifted lower and began to turn orange. A leaden atmosphere had replaced the heavy but normal silence of the hot afternoon. It made my chest heave and my scalp prickle. I'd never seen such a dead evening. The reddening sunlight didn't glitter on the conifer needles: it looked smeared on them, as with cheap poster paint. It was because the needles didn't move in the still air and because the overcast had obscured the sun's brilliance, but it seemed unnatural.

We walked for another half hour, then Alec stopped. The sun had set, and the light was beginning to fade.

"You don't know where the hell you are, do you, George?"

"We may have drifted a little to the south. We're about three ridges east of it now."

"I think you're lost."

"We'll get there tomorrow morning."

"We'd better."

We were on the edge of a little socket between two converging ridgetops. A small meadow lay at the bottom of it, palely visible, surrounded by trees. Alec said we'd spend the night there. As we descended the slope toward the meadow, there was a flash of light and a low rumble to the north.

"All I need now is a thunderstorm," said Alec.

There hadn't been any cumulonimbus clouds to the north, or in any other direction. We paused a moment in the violet light. The forest suddenly was full of patters and creaks.

"Wind's coming up."

It didn't sound like the wind; the needles weren't singing. I

194

remembered waking up one night in our house in Weaverville at what sounded like a dozen burglars walking around our living room. Too astonished for caution, I'd hurried from the bedroom, switched on the light, and found Lewis alone in the room, looking surprised. The next day I'd learned that a tremor had knocked down houses and freeway overpasses in Eureka. The vibrations from it evidently had warped the fir floorboards in my living room as shod feet do, making similar sounds.

Now it sounded like thousands of feet were hurrying around in the dark forest. As in my living room, the noise stopped abruptly after a moment. Rodrigo hissed some Spanish curses.

"Little tremor," said Alec. His voice was the tiniest bit higher pitched than usual. We stood still for several minutes, but nothing else happened. "Guess that's it. Interesting."

"There'll probably be more."

"Are you a seismologist, Carla?"

"Afraid of earthquakes, Murray?"

"I'd be a fool if I wasn't, wouldn't I?"

It was the first time Carla had spoken all afternoon. Her face was looking doughy again. I didn't suppose I looked apple cheeked either. Alec and Rodrigo looked quite ruddy.

"*Tengo hambre*," said Rodrigo.

"Nothing like a long day on the trail to work up an appetite." We crossed a little seep fringed with scarlet monkey-flowers, their blossoms almost black in the twilight, and stopped in a grove of noble fir beside the meadow. Rodrigo took a Coleman Peak lantern out of his voluminous pack and hung it from a branch, and he and Alec started making camp with almost manic energy while I sat dumbly under a tree and Carla loitered in the shadows.

"Don't wander off now, boys and girls." Alec had a lot of fancy new camping gear: I'd have been enthralled under other circumstances. He had a Firefly stove, a dome tent, and lots of other sparkly things, even waterproof matches.

"You must camp out a lot."

"Not all that much, but I like to do it right."

195

"You have a deprived childhood or something?"

"Trying to figure me out?"

"Don't you ever wonder why you're the way you are?"

"I don't have time."

"It wouldn't be fun."

"That's right. As a matter of fact, I had a very normal childhood, except that I dropped out of high school and left home when I was sixteen."

"What for?"

"You know better than that, George. It was a waste of time. I hitchhiked to Los Angeles and started a business selling game to restaurants. Branched out from there."

"Like pheasant and wild boar?"

"People like to feel aristocratic."

"Market hunting."

"Most of it's raised on farms. In fact, I got tired of it, it was so aboveboard."

"You like breaking laws, don't you?"

"Don't you? Laws are artificial."

"Nature has laws."

"Name one."

"You don't get something for nothing."

"That's the misconception that civilization is based on."

"What?"

"That humans deserve something for nothing."

"Don't you try to get something for nothing when you steal?"

"I don't steal, George. I pay for what I have."

"If you don't care about laws, why don't you like being called a thief?"

Alec didn't answer. He finished unpacking cookware and food and said something to Rodrigo, who'd been boiling water. Rodrigo started opening cans and plastic bags while Alec got a bottle of California beaujolais out of the pack.

"Set the table, George."

"What?"

"You heard me." There was even a tablecloth. I laid the aluminum plates and utensils out, feeling foolish, but I would have felt equally foolish if I'd refused. Alec opened the bottle.

"California wines are good for camping," he said. "The exercise makes them digestible, and the coarseness becomes quite enjoyable." He poured me a cup, and I drank it thirstily. I felt like grabbing the bottle and draining it. Rodrigo came over from the stove with a steaming pot of what looked like freeze-dried steaks. They smelled good. I was surprised to realize that I was hungry.

"Come and get it, Carla." Carla had sunk down under a tree. She didn't answer. We gobbled away in silence for a while. I was swallowing large hunks of meat almost unchewed. I drank two more cups of wine and began to feel pretty good.

"Hey, Carla. Carla. Oh, Carla."

"I'm not hungry."

"You'll waste away to nothing." Rodrigo said something and they both laughed, a braying horselaugh. Rodrigo said something else, then he took a steak out of the pot and walked over to Carla. He stuck it under her nose, and she recoiled from it.

"Hey, she's a vegetarian, for God's sake." Alec said something to Rodrigo, probably a translation of what I'd said. Rodrigo shrugged. He grabbed Carla by the hair and lifted her to her feet and thrust the steak in her face. She kicked at him, but he pinioned her legs against the tree and started to force her mouth open with his other hand.

I stood up, then turned to look at Alec. He grinned at me and raised his eyebrows. I ran up behind Rodrigo, grabbed him around the throat with one arm, and kidney-punched him with the other. It was like punching an oak: not quite as hard but just about as tough. For a while he didn't even react, just kept forcing Carla's jaws apart. I could see her face over his shoulder. She looked like she was at the dentist's. Then he reached around and grabbed me. I tried to avoid his hands by ducking down against his back, but he got one of them on my shoulder and started to squeeze.

The feeling went out of my arm, and my collar bone started

to bend. He got my arm off his neck and turned around. I kneed him in the groin and punched him in the stomach with my other arm. He grunted; then I felt a tremendous blow against the side of my head. He'd slapped me the way a bear slaps a hound. I clutched him, trying to stay on my feet.

Rodrigo bent over and grabbed my knee, and I felt myself being upended until I was horizontal seven feet off the ground. He'd picked me up bodily. My head hung at a strange angle, and all I could see was Coleman lantern beams prettily dappling the blue-green fir boughs above the camp. Somebody was shouting. Then Rodrigo's shaking arms bent and snapped straight, and I was flying. I saw the lamp whiz by. It seemed to be *above* me. Then I felt something very large and dark approaching very fast.

Chapter Thirty-one

I SAW A LIGHT. It hurt my head, and the pain made me feel sick. I wanted to just lie wherever I was, but there was a sense of urgency. I raised my head and tried to focus my eyes. The light was a flickering, brilliant white lantern. Alec was sitting next to it, smoking a joint. He saw me moving.

"Have a toke. It'll help your head." He extended the joint toward me, and I smelt its sweetish, charred odor. I staggered into the trees and vomited strenuously, then crouched there gasping and listening to Alec whistling softly. The sense of urgency returned, and I tottered back into the light. The sky was black above the treetops. Alec was alone in the clearing.

"Where are the others?"

"Off in the bushes somewhere."

"You son of a bitch."

"He won't kill her."

"You son of a bitch." I took a step toward him, and he produced the machine pistol again. I sat down and started to blubber.

"Oh, come on, George. It's not such a big deal. She's just an uppity cunt. Relax. Join the party."

"I'll kill him!"

"Why are you getting so excited all of a sudden? What did you expect?"

I started going through my pack, looking for my flashlight. When I found it, I ran toward the trees.

"George. Hey, George!" I kept moving. There was a burst from the pistol, incredibly loud in the silent grove, and I felt bullets snapping at the branches around me. I dived to the ground and crawled behind a tree. A powerful flashlight beam started searching for me.

"Come on, George. I'm getting tired of this." The light got brighter, and I could hear Alec's footsteps approaching. But they seemed to be coming from the wrong direction. I turned around to see if Rodrigo was coming at me from behind, but there was nobody there. Then it occurred to me that the footsteps were coming from all over the place.

The ground began to move back and forth very energetically indeed. There were accelerating and deepening booms, as though somebody was trying to start up a very large motor. I had no idea what made those sounds, but I knew what was making the crackling and crashing noises in the more immediate vicinity: falling trees. I pressed my face against the ground and sank my fingers into the duff: not a very rational response to an earthquake, since being shaken off into outer space was not a danger, but a comforting one.

I realized that I'd closed my eyes because everything turned an intense red, the color you see when there's a very bright light on the other side of your eyelids. I opened them. The grove was full of a violet-yellow glare that could have been lightning, except that it didn't quit; it just kept glaring. It *really* hurt my eyes. Then the glare coalesced into an even more brilliant azure and scarlet ball that seemed to be rolling around in the treetops, sizzling and banging like a live wire.

Alec was standing ten feet away with his back to me, looking at the azure ball. I experienced a surge of joy, a pounding sensation (my running feet), and then sharp pains in my knuckles as I drove them into the back of Alec's head. There was an explosive sound above, and the blue glare faded, but I didn't let that distract me. Alec went over like a scarecrow and didn't even try to

200

get up as I kept hitting him. I put my knee in his back and hit him some more, jabbing him with my knee for emphasis.

I felt a sharp pain at the top of my head. Somebody was pulling my hair.

"That's enough, George."

"Ahh!"

"That's enough!"

"Ah?" It was Carla. I turned around, but the camp had gone dark, and I couldn't see her face. The lantern had gone out for some reason.

"What the hell? Where's Rodrigo?"

"Never mind. Let's get out of here."

"Yeah, right."

"Have you got a flashlight?"

"Somewhere, uh." I groped around Alec and found the one he'd been using. I had no idea what I'd done with mine. I flicked it on and turned it toward Carla. She shut her eyes at the glare. Her face wasn't doughy anymore.

"You're covered with blood!"

"Come on, George."

"What about the packs?"

"Leave them." She started off into the darkness, and I followed. She was moving too fast for me; I kept stumbling. She was so far ahead that I had to keep the light high, and the ground at my feet was in darkness. She got to the slope at the other side of the grove and started to hurry up it. I told her to slow down, then my foot caught on something and I fell.

"George?"

"Yeah."

"Where's the light?"

"It went out. Wait a minute." I hadn't dropped the flashlight, luckily. I switched it on again and pointed it at the thing that had tripped me. It was Rodrigo. His face wasn't ruddy anymore.

"You cut his throat!"

"Can we *please* get out of here, George?"

201

Chapter Thirty-two

I WOKE UP PARALYZED from the nose down, with a feeling that something was watching me. I could move the tip of my nose a little, my eyelids and eyebrows, maybe my ears. The rest was like wood: wood with nerve endings. Actually the pain was encouraging. I didn't suppose I'd be feeling anything if I really was paralyzed. Spending the night out in the mountains without a sleeping bag doesn't paralyze you, it just stiffens you.

As I said, I could open my eyes easily enough, but the information this provided was limited. I could see the back of Carla's head, some needle-covered ground, and some fir foliage in the background. I recalled the previous night and suddenly felt more limber. The endocrine system is a wonderful thing. I tensed for a moment, then jumped up and whirled around, coming face to face with a medium-size bear that was peeking at us from behind a fir sapling a dozen feet away. It looked utterly appalled, turned, and gave me a very brief glimpse of its hindquarters.

"Crash, crash, *crash!*" Then silence. Carla stirred and moaned.

"What are you jumping around for?" she said in a peevish, faraway voice. She must have been dreaming. Then she went tense and rolled onto her elbows. "What was that!"

"Just a bear."

"How do you know?"

"I saw it."

She shook her head and rubbed her face. Little flecks of dried blood fell off it. Her hair was matted with black clots. She shivered.

"Ugh!"

"We'd feel better if we'd brought a sleeping bag."

"I told you, I've got a cache at the swamp with spare bags and food."

"Are you sure we're headed in the right direction?"

"Yes, we'll be there in a few hours."

"How can you be so sure?"

"Did anyone ever tell you about the stars, George? You can tell direction by them."

"The stars aren't out now."

"They were last night."

"Yes, but—."

"Just be quiet for a minute." She ran a hand through her hair and caught a finger in a blood clot. "I've *got* to get to some water."

I saw her point, though the thought of a cold bath didn't appeal at that moment. The ridgetop hollow where we'd lain down exhausted after traveling several hours from Alec's camp was still full of morning chill and damp, although the sunlight was climbing down from the treetops. Carla tucked her torn shirt into her jeans and started up the slope. I wondered where she got her energy after eating nothing for the past twenty-four hours.

The sunlight on the ridgetop felt wonderful at first, but after a couple of hours of walking without water, it began to be too much of a good thing. I was glad when a high haze began to filter it a little. It was still warm and humid. I found a few ripe raspberries, but Carla kept hurrying along. It was a relief when she finally turned off the ridgetop, though I didn't look forward to eventually climbing out of the steep canyon she led me into. When we were about two-thirds of the way to the bottom, she stopped and turned to me.

'Do you hear that?"

"What?"

"Listen."

"I hear the creek."

"It sounds like it's in flood. It shouldn't be making so much noise at this time of year." I could see what she meant when we got to the canyon bottom. The creek wasn't really flooding—it wasn't full of silt and overflowing its banks—but it wasn't the limpid string of green pools and riffles you'd expect in summer. The water was dark and opaque. "The earthquake must have changed the ground-water patterns."

"Is that possible?"

"I don't know, George. I'm not a geologist."

"What was all that with the booming and the colored lights, anyway?"

"Earthquakes release a lot of energy."

"I'll say."

"I'm going to take a bath."

"Looks awfully cold."

Carla started to unbutton her shirt, then looked at me. "George?"

"What?"

"Would you mind?"

"Mind? Oh." I wandered into the alder thickets downstream, feeling obtuse and rejected. I climbed past some boulders, undressed, and hopped very quickly in and out of a sandy cove. It was full of yellow-striped garter snakes, surprisingly lively in the chill water. I thought of *The Rime of the Ancient Mariner*, where the albatross drops off the hero's neck when he blesses the sea snakes playing around the ghost ship.

"George!" I hurried back upstream and found Carla sitting on a rock, much cleaner.

"What's wrong?"

"Nothing. I guess I'm nervous."

"Me too."

"Look, I'm sorry I called you a fool."

"That's all right."

"No, I should have trusted you."

"I didn't trust myself all that much." I put my hand on her shoulder, and she grasped it for a moment, then let go of it. She looked across the creek and kicked at the sand with her boot. "You want to talk about it?"

"Talk about what?"

"Last night."

"Not particularly."

"You might feel better."

"I picked up a dissecting knife while Alec had us in my study. Didn't you see me?"

"No."

"I thought you did. Being a biologist comes in handy once in a while."

"Wow. Deadlier than the male."

"That's bullshit, George."

Chapter Thirty-three

IT TOOK A LITTLE MORE than two hours to get to the swamp. It was past noon when we came to the gully up which I'd first reached it.

"Hey, I recognize this."

"Damn," Carla said.

"What's the matter now?"

"It's not running."

"Doesn't it dry up in the summer?"

We were talking about the little creek at the bottom of the gully. There were a few pools, and the streambed was still damp, but there wasn't any flow, not above ground anyway.

"Not like this." She started running. I trudged along after her, and in about fifteen minutes reached the level area and the huge trees. Everything seemed unchanged: same willows and grass where her tent had been, same marshy area beyond. I followed the path to the bathing pool and found Carla standing beside it. She looked stricken, and when I got closer I could see why. The pool was empty, not only of dragons, but of water.

"It's dried up."

"What about the other pools?"

"The whole damned thing. Look at it."

I did, and what had seemed the same began to look different. The lilies and cobra plants were leaning over, and some were wilted. Patches of rush and sedge looked trampled, and the very ground level seemed to have sunk. There was a muddy smell that I didn't remember from before.

"They're all gone."

"The dragons?"

"I looked in every pool. They're all gone."

I looked at the mud at the bottom of the empty pool. It was starting to dry, and even crack, in spots. The log I'd sat on stuck into it at a grotesque angle, looking very dead and ponderous now that it no longer floated.

"They must be around somewhere."

"Where do you think they are, George?"

"It's no use getting mad at *me*."

"I'm not getting mad at you. I'm just not in the mood for idle babbling."

"Can we have something to eat?"

"I'm not hungry."

"You're going to get sick if you don't eat. You haven't eaten for over twenty-four hours."

"So what?"

"Well, can *I* eat something?"

"Help yourself."

"Help myself to *what*?"

"Oh, all right." She turned abruptly and led me to a small log structure built into the slope above the swamp. I'd never noticed it. We pulled some logs away from the front, revealing a small chamber that contained two old sleeping bags and boxes of canned goods, matches, and other supplies.

"How did you get all this stuff in here?"

"A little at a time."

I rummaged through one of the boxes. Applesauce, peaches, sardines, crackers, deviled ham. Deviled ham? "I thought you were a vegetarian?"

"It's an emergency supply. I'm not a Jain."

"A what?"

"I thought you went to college."

"I did. What's a Jain?"

"A member of a nonviolent Indian sect."

"Well, you're certainly not a Jain."

"Screw you."

"More like a Sikh."

"It's lucky for you if I am, isn't it?"

"Uh, got a can opener?"

"Hm."

"Shit."

"Keep your pants on, George." She rummaged through another box and found one. I'd already opened a tin of sardines by that time. I started eating them with my fingers.

"Have some. Fish aren't the same as meat."

"All right."

I began to feel better with every bite. Carla opened a can of mixed fruit, and we had some of that. The sugar made me positively euphoric.

"What about the caves?"

"I thought of the caves, George."

"Well, what about them?"

"We didn't find any caves, remember?"

"Maybe an entrance opened up. The water must have gone down. Maybe it opened an entrance as it receded."

"I didn't see any."

"Did you look where we'd dug? How about under the log that we wedged down into the bottom of the pool so we could stay underwater to dig?"

"I looked in all the pools, George."

"You couldn't have looked very hard."

"Oh, leave me alone." She thumped down the fruit can and stalked back toward the swamp. I made a face, finished the sardines, then finished the fruit. I could have eaten more, but I decided not to overdo it.

Somehow I couldn't feel too bad about the dragons at the moment. I had food in my stomach, a warm sleeping bag, and I was alive. It just didn't seem possible that one lousy earthquake could wipe out a species, and if it did, that was natural, wasn't it? It wasn't our fault, so why should we feel bad about it? I could understand how Carla felt, of course, but she was probably being too pessimistic.

I began to get drowsy, a nice, well-fed sort of drowsiness. It was just the right temperature in the shade of the giant trees: not too cool, not too warm. The mosquitoes weren't bothering me. I wondered if the drying of the swamp had extirpated them. I lay down on the deep, soft needle duff at the base of a giant pine. A dragonfly flew up, making a rustling sound with its wings, and landed on the tip of my boot. It didn't seem concerned that its swamp had disappeared. After it flew away, the grove became quite still. I looked up at the sky a little while, then closed my eyes.

I was standing on a trail alongside a steep, rather barren canyon. There were a few spindly pines and bushes and a lot of yellow and reddish brown rocks. I had the impression that I'd just made a long journey on the trail and had returned to my starting point. I looked toward a narrow ravine that opened up the canyon from the trail. A giant was standing in it with his back to me, towering like a tree above the top of the ravine.

The giant was a little like the spectral colossi in Goya's etchings, but he wasn't brutish like them. He was slender, even spidery. There was something of the thoroughbred about him. He was a handsome buckskin color, with gracefully defined muscles and a mane of darker hair that continued down his spine.

He turned around, and I saw his face. He had a low forehead, receding chin, broad nose, high cheekbones, and small eyes, but he didn't really look simian. He had full lips, which apes don't have. He didn't look human either. His face was the same buckskin color as the rest of him, and I had the impression that he was entirely covered with short, coarse hair, like a horse. He didn't appear to see me. I stood motionless, enthralled, as he turned away and moved up the ravine with a nimble gait that reminded me of a daddy longlegs climbing a wall.

I felt a pain behind my ear and thought for a moment that

209

Carla was pulling my hair again, but it was a different kind of pain, a push instead of a pull. It was something cold and hard. I opened my eyes and saw fir needles and a withered pinedrop plant. I'd rolled over onto my side in my sleep.

"Don't move," said Alec.

Chapter Thirty-four

W HERE'S Carla?"
"I don't know. Ow!"
"I told you not to dick around with me, George. You should have killed me when you had the chance."
"Don't thank me, thank Carla."
"You're lucky I'm not a cruel and vindictive man."
"Lucky like Blackwell?"
"He didn't feel a thing. Now where is the bitch?"
There was something strange about his voice. I turned my head to look at him. He jammed the pistol against it again, but I got a glance. One side of his face was purple and swollen, the eye shut tight. The other side was dead white, and the eye was opened so wide that it seemed to bulge. Flies buzzed around the back of his head and neck.
"My God, you should be in a hospital. How did you get here?"
"I walked. Don't worry about me, George. I'm harder to kill than musclebound Guatemalans."
"I didn't kill him. Carla did."
"I don't care who killed him. Call her."
"She's not here." He jabbed the pistol at me again, and the sight cut the sensitive skin behind my ear. I felt a trickle of blood run down my neck, pause at the shoulder, then continue down the shoulder blade. It tickled. "Call her yourself."

I felt him tense. I took a good look at the sky and the trees. I supposed it was better than looking at a hospital wall. But he stood up and backed away from me.

"Let's go find her."

"Find her yourself."

"Come on, George. You don't want me to do that." He was right. I stood up. "Where did you get that?"

"Get what?"

Alec kicked the empty fruit can. "She has a hidey-hole here, doesn't she?" He pressed the gun into my right kidney. "Where's her hidey-hole?"

"She kept a few canned goods in a hollow tree."

"Never mind, I see it." Alec marched me to Carla's cache, visible through the trees, and made me turn it inside out in front of him.

"No maps here, Alec. She keeps the copies she made of them in her safe deposit box in Cave Junction."

"You wouldn't tell me that if she did, George. Stop slipping and sliding. Just do what I tell you."

"Why'd you make the maps if you're so smart? Into keeping records, like Eichmann?"

"Why aren't you rich if you're so smart? Thorough paperwork is the key to profits. You'd be surprised how few really safe places there are to dispose of hazardous materials."

"How did Tom find them if they were so safe?"

"He wouldn't have found anything if it wasn't for the goddamned coyotes. And goddamned lazy Rodrigo."

"What?"

Alec didn't answer. He gestured toward the swamp. "What's down there?"

"A bunch of empty holes."

"What?" I told him what had happened to the swamp.

"You expect me to believe that?"

"See for yourself."

We walked down to the swamp, Alec staying several steps

212

behind me. The pools were still empty and even drier than before.

"Where'd the water go?"

"Into the ground."

"There must have been some kind of cavity down there for it to disappear so quickly. Caves. I bet there are caves down there."

"Could be."

"I bet Carla's in the caves."

"We didn't find any caves."

"You didn't find any while you were snoring under that tree. Maybe Carla did. Let's look."

Alec forced me to lead him from pool to pool as he methodically examined even the shallowest ones. Flies were starting to buzz around my neck now, and the mosquitoes were active again. The smell of the drying mud was strong in the midafternoon heat. Alec didn't seem to mind any of this.

"How come you keep avoiding that place, George?"

"What place?" Alec pointed. "There's nothing there."

"Let's look." We pushed past an azalea thicket to the pool Carla and I had dug out. A rope was tied to a nearby Port Orford cedar. It led to the bottom of the pool and disappeared under the log we'd wedged there. Carla had found an entrance. She'd even made a kind of walkway of fir branches to the hole so you wouldn't have to get your boots muddy on the pool's bottom.

"Let's go get a flashlight."

"You want to climb down there?"

"That's right."

"Why don't we just wait until she comes out?"

"I want to see what's down there." It also would save him the trouble of burying us, I thought. He marched me back to the tree, where he'd left Rodrigo's pack. He took out a flashlight, a couple of plastic jars, and a day pack, then put the jars in the day pack and handed it to me.

"What's this for?"

"Specimens."

"Specimens?"

"Stop being obtuse, George. If these creatures lived in the pools, they must be in the caves now. I came here to get specimens, and I'm damned well going to get specimens. I *always* accomplish my goals." Alec took out another plastic jar, a smaller one, and sniffed a little white powder from it. "This stuff is very useful in tight spots, if you have the willpower not to abuse it." He offered the jar to me. I shook my head. "It'll make things easier."

"Did you offer Tom some before you shot him?"

"I didn't need to offer any to Tom. Tom was always well supplied—with everything except willpower. Who said anything about shooting, anyway? I need you to carry the specimens. I've got nothing against you. I wouldn't have killed Tom if he'd just given me back the maps and promised to be good. I don't even kill snakes if they bite me, as long as I know they've used up their venom."

"How many times have you been bitten by snakes?"

"Oh, three or four."

Chapter Thirty-five

I T DIDN'T LOOK like much of a cave entrance. If it hadn't been for Carla's rope disappearing into it, I'd have taken it for a shadow or a shallow depression in the mud. You had to stick your head into it and crane your neck to see how it led down into the darkness. It was very dark darkness when you did see it, very dark indeed. Alec took a look and motioned me to go first. Then he changed his mind and stopped me.

"Turn out your pockets, George." I did. Wallet and keys. Alec took a roll of nylon twine out of his pocket and knotted it around my waist carefully. He payed out about a dozen feet of it and attached the other end loosely to his belt. "Just to make sure you don't get lost."

"What am I going to do down there without a flashlight?"

"Safety first."

Alec squatted on the fir boughs watching me as I wriggled feet first into the hole. It wasn't easy. When I was all the way in except my head, he smiled.

"Tight spot."

"Ha ha."

"Just watch out and we'll come back okay."

I pulled my head under, and the world contracted to a patch of greenish yellow light overhead. It was a strange sensation. The hole was very steep, more a chimney than a passage. I had to brace myself against the rock walls and inch my way down. It seemed to be a large crack in the bedrock, though it was so slimy with ooze that little rock was exposed. It felt grainy, though not as much as sandstone. Some kind of volcanic deposit, as Carla had said.

It got steeper and narrower, then opened out again a little, enough to turn around in. The patch of daylight overhead dis-appeared as Alec came swarming busily after me. His flashlight didn't help me much. If I looked up, it dazzled my eyes; if I looked down, I saw mostly the shadows that I cast by interrupting the flashlight beam. I had to move faster than I liked to stay very far ahead of Alec, but I did anyway. I wanted to keep out of range of his boots.

As I descended, I passed other cracks that led sideways from the main one. None were big enough to squeeze into. It was just as well: side passages in a place like this didn't appeal to me. Of course, we had Carla's rope to follow, although it gave no sign that someone was at the other end of it, no twitchings or tautness.

Below me Alec's flashlight beam faded into a vaporous black-ness. It seemed as though we might as well have been climbing off the lower edge of the world into outer space. My breath swirled and billowed in the light. I wished I'd worn warmer clothes: my knees, back, and elbows were already getting numb from contact with the damp stone, not to mention scraped raw from its coarseness. I wanted to rest, but Alec kept on coming. I wished I'd taken some of his white powder.

Finally I saw something below, a pebbly floor, dry and rela-tively clean. I hoped this would be the end of it, so we could turn around and climb back to the light. I inched down the last dozen feet and touched my soles to the pebbles with gratitude. Beyond the circle of Alec's flashlight was only more blackness. I reached out and touched empty blackness all around me.

Alec dropped out of the crack and shone his flashlight around. We were in a low-ceilinged gallery that extended as far as the flashlight's beam in all directions. The rope snaked off along the floor, disappearing into blackness. We crouched in silence for a little while, listening. Water was trickling somewhere far away; otherwise, I heard only the ringing of my ears.

"What if there's another tremor?"

"What if there is? Doesn't seem to have done any damage here. It's unlikely anyway." Alec's voice sounded even stranger down here, echoing dully off unseen surfaces.

We started following the rope through the gallery. The ceiling was only about three feet high, so we had to scramble along hunched over, ape-fashion. I glimpsed something at the edge of the flashlight beam and veered aside to investigate. A swarm of pale pink centipedes was feeding on something. They made a rustling sound, audible as I got closer. They swarmed so thickly that I first thought they were a single organism, a real nightmare of the deep, but they were just smallish cave centipedes, ordinary-looking enough as individuals. It was a little strange that they'd already gotten so deep into a cave that had been filled with water the day before.

"Interesting," said Alec, "there must have been dry pockets among all these cracks." He brushed the centipedes aside (they showed no fear of us, probably never having encountered humans before) and revealed a shriveled amphibian shape. "They're down here all right."

"Carla thinks they breed down here."

Alec prodded the shape. It was gray and deliquescent. "Can't tell if this is an adult or a larva." He took a vial out of his pocket and put some of the centipedes in it. "This may be an unclassified species."

"You won't get money for it."

"How can you tell? Knowledge is power."

The gallery continued level for a little longer, then began to slope downward. The roof receded, allowing us to walk upright but walking became harder because the floor was increasingly littered with slimy rock debris. I wondered uneasily where the shattered rocks had come from.

"Do you think the earthquake shook these down from the ceiling?"

"Some of them, maybe."

217

"This thing could go on for miles."

"Just follow the rope, George."

The rope came to a perpendicular rock wall and ran off along it to the right. We followed. It was nice to have a boundary. I'd begun to lose my sense of direction in the all-pervading blackness. Sometimes I couldn't tell if the slope was going up or down. The slippery slope.

It began to get steeper, so that we had to lower ourselves carefully. We were more and more coated with icy mud. It was a good place to get hypothermia. The downslope ended in an upslope, and the rope turned again and continued downward in the trough between the two slopes. It was like climbing down a gully. There were some pretty big boulders in it, not easy to climb over, particularly since some had pools of water below them. Alec shined his flashlight in the black water, but we couldn't see anything in it except some small white amphipods.

The sounds of water that we'd heard first in the gallery had been getting louder. Now they took on a greater intensity, perhaps from being contained by the rock walls of the trough. Then I noticed something that increased my nervousness.

"This water is starting to have a current." Alec played the flashlight on a pool. There was a lazy movement to the surface of the water that hadn't been there farther up the trough.

"So what?"

"What if the groundwater level is changing again? Rising?"

"Then we'll climb out."

"What if it's rising fast?"

"You have a melodramatic imagination, George."

"I'm wet enough already."

"I don't think we have much farther to go."

We started finding more dead salamanders, some draped on bare rock, some floating in the sluggishly flowing water.

"I guess you're right," said Alec.

"What?"

"It's rising. They wouldn't be floating otherwise. They're larvae, see? They must have been stranded and died when the water receded, then started to float when it rose again. If the pools had been here the whole time, there'd still be some alive."

"They might all have been killed by a shock wave before the water receded. I've heard that can happen in underwater earthquakes."

"Sounds like wishful thinking to me, George." Alec was right. Another few dozen feet down the trough we came to a sheet of black water. Carla's rope ran to the edge of it, then continued, floating, as far as the flashlight beam would reach. The water was encroaching visibly on the rocks, swallowing a pebble here, a patch of mud there.

Chapter Thirty-six

T HIS IS FAR ENOUGH," said Alec. He flashed the light in my eyes. I threw myself backward, which would have been a futile gesture if Alec hadn't tied us together with nylon twine. The pull of my movement jarred him before the twine came loose from his belt. It was enough to upset his aim with the pistol and to take the flashlight beam off me for a moment.

I rushed him, but I wasn't getting him from behind this time. He hit me in the temple with the flashlight as I plowed into him, and I slipped on the stones and fell. When I opened my eyes again, it was dark. I heard Alec breathing hard and scrabbling in the stones. He'd either broken the flashlight on my head or dropped it.

I heard a metallic sound and rolled away from it, then curled up in a ball as bullets began bouncing off the rocks around me. Bullets acquire a life of their own when they ricochet: they buzz around like lead and brass bees, looking for somebody to sting. It's best to stay still.

The firing stopped, and Alec grunted. There were shuffling sounds, then silence. I crouched in the darkness for a long time, visualizing Alec crouched a few yards away so vividly that I thought I heard him several times. Then I felt a chill soaking into my boots. I reached back and touched water. The devil and the deep blue sea.

I couldn't move up or down, so I tried moving sideways. I inched along the rising water's edge crab-fashion, groping blindly for Carla's rope. It took an unbelievably long time, but I finally located it. When I picked it up, it felt oddly light. I forced myself not to pull on it in a panic, to follow it slowly and carefully away from the water. I didn't get far before I came to the end, where Alec had cut it and dragged the other end behind him as he started back to the surface.

I think that if Alec had left his gun behind I would have shot myself at that moment. I almost wished I'd let him shoot me. The death awaiting me now would be a much more arduous one. I would spend hours scrambling over the slimy rocks before the water rose sufficiently to trap me against the cave ceiling and then drown me, or before I collapsed from exhaustion and hypothermia.

I wanted to rush off and look for the other end of the rope, but I knew Alec would have carried it a good distance away, and I forced myself to sit still. At least I had some idea where I was. I groped around the rocks for another excessively long period and found the flashlight.

I flipped the switch with trembling fingers. It was dead. Alec wouldn't have left it behind otherwise. I jiggled it and flipped the switch again, still with no effect, then unscrewed the top, switched the batteries, moistened the terminals, and tightened the bulb. I screwed the top back on and flipped the switch again. Nothing. I suppressed an urge to throw the thing away and tried gently turning it, bulb end down. A pale orange glow weakly illuminated the rock I was crouching over. There were scuff marks on it, and a small drop of blood.

Alec and I had left a pretty clear trail as we clambered over the muddy rocks. If we hadn't, I'd have been doomed. By holding the flashlight a few inches above the ground, I was able to follow the trail, not quickly, but fairly steadily, though I had to stop and backtrack a few times. The blood helped, small drops or spatters every few yards. Alec apparently had been hit by one of his ricochets, at least superficially.

Still, I wasn't moving fast enough. The flow of water down the trough was increasing markedly. It was beginning to obliterate footprints and skid marks. It was beginning to splash and roar over the boulder around which I had to climb. A deeper roaring also was increasing behind me, or was it above? It was hard to tell where sounds came from in the rock-strewn blackness.

I made it to the top of the gullylike trough and realized that my problems had hardly begun. It would be much harder to follow the trail over the jumbled rocks of the slope than it had been along the narrow bottom of the trough. At least I'd be free of water, I thought; but after I'd climbed a few yards up the slope, the flashlight suddenly was reflected in a little rivulet, half visible under the stones. I heard a pattering sound to one side, turned the light on it, and saw a string of drops descending from above.

I began to get clumsy. The numbness from the cold had receded as I struggled up the steep trough, but as I hesitated now, it seeped back into shaking muscles. My feet and hands were cold to the bone. I had to slow down to keep from falling among the uneven rocks. I was afraid of dropping the flashlight, but I didn't dare to stop and rest. Another string of drops from above splashed my face and stung my eyes. I had to stop and wait for them to clear. I could see little enough in the weak flashlight beam, but one blind step could be the end of me.

I began to get irrational. I realized that I was whistling "Dancing in the Dark," and I had no idea how long I'd been doing it. I realized that the flashlight was shining on rope, and that I had no idea how long I'd carefully been following it as though it was a trail of footprints on the rock. I grabbed it and then almost dropped it, afraid I'd find that Alec had cut this segment too. It seemed a fearsome temptation to pull on it. I weighed it gingerly in my hand: it seemed heavy. I pulled: it seemed taut. I had a sudden vision of Alec pulling on the other end, single eye glaring in the dark, and it seemed so absolutely real that I flinched and crouched.

The shock of that cleared my head for a moment. I turned the flashlight off, stuck it carefully in my pocket, and started following the rope hand over hand. I thought I could save the batteries that way. Maybe I wasn't really thinking that clearly: I took five hasty steps and fell headlong on the rocks. I got up again and started feeling my way more carefully, a step at a time. I was still whistling. It seemed a waste of energy, and I stopped; but a moment later I found that I was doing it again, so I gave up trying to control my mouth and concentrated on my feet. I shivered, babbled, and whistled my way up the slope.

My shoulder bumped against something sharp. It hurt, and I whimpered. There was a rock wall to my right now. That was nice: it saved me the trouble of moving in *that* direction. I heard a roaring in front of me but paid no attention to it. I knew directions were meaningless in this place. I just followed the rope, nice taut rope, and suddenly found myself up to my thighs in water so fast that without the rope to hang onto it would have swept me away. It merely swept me off my feet.

I floundered upright and braced myself against the current and against a desire to let go of the rope. It was just too much to bear, and I sobbed a couple of times in heartfelt sorrow for myself. But the water was too cold to stay in. I took a step forward, and it didn't get any deeper; so I took more steps, and it got shallower. I splashed along a little farther and scraped my head painfully on a rock ceiling. I tried to *kick* the ceiling, though fortunately not hard enough to upend myself onto the rocks. I floundered a few feet more, scramped my head again, floundered a few feet more, scraped my head, and came to the conclusion that it would be helpful to walk stooped over.

It was harder to walk in that position. I didn't like it. I didn't seem to be making much progress; in fact, I wondered if I was moving forward at all. Maybe I was just walking in place, and the *rope* was moving. Suddenly it felt scaly and sinuous, alive. I dropped it, rubbed my eyes, slapped myself on top of the head, and picked it up again. Just a rope.

I was walking in water. *That* was why the movement had

seemed strange. Or had I been in water when the rope had turned into a snake? It hadn't turned into a snake, of course. I would have liked to sit down and think about how I'd gotten into the water again, but it was getting above my knees, so that wasn't practical. It wasn't really that hard to walk in. It seemed to have less current now, more buoyancy. It wasn't so cold anymore either.

I found that I didn't need to put my feet down on the rocks so carefully anymore. The water buoyed me up. Sometimes I could just kick with my feet and pull myself along on the rope. That was a relief, though it was getting a little hard to move my arms and legs. I decided to take a rest, but then my head scraped the ceiling again, and I felt angry. I wasn't even standing upright and my head was scraping the ceiling. Then I felt frightened: I realized my head had scraped the ceiling because the water was up to my chest. I took the rope and looped and knotted it around my wrist. It was important to hold onto the rope, for some reason.

I scraped my head several more times, so that I stopped being afraid and started feeling angry again. It was such a burning, punishing sensation to scrape against the hard rock, to be above the water. On the other hand, my body under the water felt cool and pleasant. I scraped my head again, then ducked it petulantly underwater. But I couldn't breathe water. I thrust my head out again and took a gasp of air. It was painful: it burned my lungs. It didn't seem to do me any good.

Water would cool my lungs. Dragons breathed water. I realized that there were dragons around me in the water. I could feel them brushing against my face and shoulders in the darkness. Actually, it wasn't that dark in the water. There was a light. I couldn't tell where it was coming from, somewhere deeper in the water. It was a cool light, but bright. I couldn't tell just what color it was. There was yellow in it, and blue.

I felt a hand on my shoulder and saw that Alec was there with the dragons, apparently breathing water too.

224

"Breathe water and you can speak to the dragons," he said "They'll speak to you."

"What will they say?" I felt skeptical, nervous. It was a strange idea.

"They'll say—." Alec moved his lips in a language I couldn't understand.

"What?"

"You have to breathe water." It seemed sensible, and I began to get excited at the prospect of learning this new language. I felt so excited that I kicked out with my feet and swam forward some more.

"Watch out," said Alec, "you'll kick me."

"Sorry."

"We'd better talk about this. We have to make full use of this opportunity." This seemed like a good idea, but I wanted to pull myself just a little farther along the rope. As Alec had said, you have to accomplish your goals. So I pulled myself a little farther and enjoyed the sense of accomplishment that followed, and took a deep breath of the cool, luminous water.

Chapter Thirty-seven

I WAS VOMITING. It seemed that I'd spent an awful lot of time vomiting lately. It wasn't very stylish. And this was *really* vomiting, a vomit to end all vomits. In fact, nobody could vomit like this and live. I was vomiting up my stomach and intestines. Not only stomach and intestines: heart, liver, lungs, testicles, legs, arms, head. I was going to turn myself inside out vomiting. That would be a kind of record. George Kilgore, the human sea cucumber. But I couldn't live like that, inside out; I'd have to die. That would be nice. No more vomiting.

I decided that I must be inside out already because I seemed to be vomiting *backward*. A disagreeable pressure was pouring into my mouth. I pushed against it, but it persisted, and eventually it got to be too much work, and I relaxed and let it flow into me until my ribs ached. Then the pressure stopped, and I deflated like a balloon. It started again, and I decided it wasn't so bad. I let myself be inflated and deflated a number of times, and it got to be rather pleasant. I felt like one of those balloons I had when I was a kid that had grinning faces printed on them. The bigger you blew the balloon, the bigger the grin got. When the pressure stopped, I was annoyed. I opened my eyes to complain. A dazzle of light hurt them, and I closed them again.

"George!" A woman's voice.

"Um." I swallowed. It hurt. I felt that I was strangling,

226

choked, coughed, retched, and finally got a breath. I opened my eyes again. By squinting I could see trees, sky, and somebody's head.

"Are you all right?"

"All right?"

"I pulled you out on the rope. It started jerking when the pool was filling with water, so I pulled it and you popped up like a fish! God, you were blue."

"Alec."

"What about him?"

"Where is he?"

"I don't know. There's a pack here. What happened?"

"I don't know." I closed my eyes. It occurred to me that I felt very bad. My heart was beating painfully, and I could hardly move. The warmth of the sleeping bag Carla had wrapped me in felt good, though. I was sleepy suddenly.

"George?"

"What happened to *you*?"

"What do you mean?"

"Didn't you see us down there?"

"No."

"We followed your rope. Where were you?"

"I followed some side passages on the way back to look for dragons. You must have passed me."

"Find any?"

"No living ones."

"I want to sleep now."

The last rays of sunlight were hitting the treetops when I awoke again. Clouds of midges danced in them, and I lay and watched them for a while, until the light faded and I couldn't see them anymore. A robin sang, good old suburban robin. It stopped, made a querulous sound, and swooped down over my head. I sat up and watched it land beside the pool. It ran around picking at the ground, evidently scavenging things thrown up when the water resurged and overflowed.

Carla was gone. I hauled myself carefully out of the sleeping bag. I was pale, sore, and lightheaded, but ambulatory, except that Carla had taken my clothes off. I looked around and found them hanging from a bush, more or less dry. I put them on.

I walked over to the pool, ignoring the robin's protests, and looked in. The bottom was obscured, but the silt already was settling out of the upper levels. I didn't see anything alive in it, though. I walked around, looking for Carla. Alec's pack still leaned against the tree where he'd left it. I found myself veering away from it almost involuntarily, as though something might jump out at me if I even touched it.

Carla wasn't at her old campsite. I followed the path to the swimming pool and found her sitting on the boulder. She looked pale, grayish, but I supposed the absence of sunlight contributed to that.

"You didn't find any living dragons down there, did you, George?"

"No."

"I guess they're all dead."

"Really?"

"The shock wave from the earthquake must have killed them all immediately."

"But there've been earthquakes here before."

"Where are they, then?" She waved at the silted, lifeless pool.

"They might still be down there. What about all that water down at the bottom? Wait until the water clears before you give up."

"I don't know, George. I'm tired. I'm going to sleep." She started back toward the campsite.

"Don't you want to eat?"

"No."

"You'll feel better."

"I don't *want* to feel better." She took a sleeping bag into the shadow of the trees and climbed into it, removing only her boots. If there'd been a wall available, she would have turned her face to it. I wasn't that hungry either, but I had some more sardines and made some tea with a pot I found in Carla's cache. Then I sat against a tree as the stars came out. I'd been feeling pretty good—glad to be alive—but now my spirits faded with the last daylight.

It seemed incredible that the dragons could be gone so abruptly. I felt a dull vacuity. Before, it had seemed easier that they'd vanished from a natural force: now it seemed unfair that there was nobody to blame. I wondered if a few might have survived the earthquake if Blackwell hadn't stolen the specimens he'd planted in Limestone Creek. It would have been nice to fill the vacuity with righteous anger, but I couldn't pump any up. It would have been nice to be as indifferent to the dragons' fate as Alec had assured me the dragons were themselves, but I couldn't be that either. I hovered in gray regret.

I thought of Alec, floating indifferently in the dark water below. Or was he? I understood why we tie up the dead in cloth and bury them in wood under stones. I wished there was a stone over the cave opening. I was glad, anyway, that Carla's rope was coiled beside the pool now, no longer reaching down into the blackness.

A waxing moon rose in the east, hardly more than a sliver, but welcome. I thought of building a fire, but it seemed too much effort. It would only prolong the night. I wanted the night to end so I could go away. I took my boots off and got into the sleeping bag, which I'd fetched unwillingly from beside the cave pool. I wasn't sleeping beside the cave pool. As I lay there, I heard a scolding whisper and saw a faint gray shape streak across the stars. The flying squirrels were still here anyway.

I dozed off quickly and must have slept several hours, but then had to struggle up from a suffocating dream of black water and bloodless, grimacing faces. The pulse pounding in my ears made a high-pitched, disagreeable sound: "sleet, sleet, sleet." If I closed my eyes, the water and faces would reappear, and my heart would start to race, so I just lay awake for a long time, watching moon shadows slide across the grove. Crickets were singing again, feebly. It was a chill, damp night.

I slept again at last and dreamed of water again, but not so

229

nastily. I wasn't in it but standing against a rock wall, hearing the water trickle within, a faint sound that disquieted, but didn't frighten, me. It made me curious, so much so that I awoke again. The moon was directly overhead.

Something *was* moving beside my ear, so quietly that I felt as much as heard it. It wasn't water; it had the slightly scratchy complexity of life, of respiration, irritability. I turned my head and saw faintly, but unmistakably, in the weak moonlight, a dragon. It was about three inches from my nose, making its imperturbable, wind-up walking movements. It began to veer away, disturbed at the turning of my head. I grabbed it, a little roughly in my excitement, so that it wriggled and made a small gasping noise. I relaxed my grip a little but held it firmly.

I stumbled into my boots and ran to where Carla was sleeping. Moonlight is deceptive: she wasn't where I thought she was. I crashed around in the bushes, and she was already sitting up when I found her.

"What the hell are you doing, George?"

I held the dragon up in the moonlight so she could see it, then handed it to her. I was pretty sure there were more of them around. You never see the *last* of a vanishing species, not in the wild anyway. Rarity grades imperceptibly into nonentity.

"They must have come out of the water before the tremor," said Carla. "They must have been down gopher holes the whole time."

"Sounds reasonable. Animals foretell earthquakes. How come you didn't think of that?"

"I did think of it, George. Was I supposed to go digging at random?"

"Just asking."

One doesn't often get to make such a presentation, and I was feeling dewy eyed; but Carla didn't jump up and down, which didn't surprise me, knowing Carla. Still, she held the impatient little creature for a moment before setting it back on its rubber legs. It toddled into the darkness, heading for the pools.